Murder at the Book Club

By

Betsy Reavley

D0611696

Copyright © 2018 Betsy Reavley

The right of Betsy Reavley to be identified as the Author of the Work has been asserted by her in accordance Copyright, Designs and Patents Act 1988.

First published in 2018 by Bloodhound Books

Apart from any use permitted under UK copyright law, this publication may only be reproduced, stored, or transmitted, in any form, or by any means, with prior permission in writing of the publisher or, in the case of reprographic production, in accordance with the terms of licences issued by the Copyright Licensing Agency.

All characters in this publication are fictitious and any resemblance to real persons, living or dead, is purely coincidental.

www.bloodhoundbooks.com

Print ISBN 978-1-912604-70-8

Also By Betsy Reavley

Beneath The Watery Moon

Carrion

The Quiet Ones

The Optician's Wife

Frailty

Pressure

Praise For Betsy Reavley

"Holy freaking hell Betsy is back with a new psychological thriller and she is on fire!" **Shell Baker - Chelle's Book Reviews**

"The plotting is excellent and the pacing spot-on. A deep sense of foreboding and growing peril permeates the entire novel." **Mark Wilson - Author**

"PRESSURE by Betsy Reavley is a unique and utterly compelling thriller that will suck you in from the very beginning and drag you down into its murky depths along with its characters." **Linda Green - Books Of All Kinds**

"A captivating, chilling, at times gruesome thriller by our own lady of suspense: Betsy Reavley!" **Caroline Vincent - Bits About Books**

"A super-fast paced thriller that I felt I had to read just as fast, as if my own reading-oxygen was in short supply." **Michelle Ryles - The Book Magnet**

"This book is such a creepy thrill ride, I was just blown away from the very beginning." **Ashley Gillan - (e)Book Nerd Reviews**

"Intense, toe curling, action packed, spine tingling, and absolutely brilliant." **Kaisha Holloway - The Writing Garnet**

"The pacing of the story is really good especially if you prefer a character driven story with twists strategically placed to really catch you out." **Rachel Broughton - Rae Reads**."

"Bursting with suspense and intrigue, Pressure is an atmospheric thriller that'll keep you glued to the pages and guessing right to the end." **Aileen Mckenzie - Feminisia Libros Reviews**

"Pressure is the ultimate locked room mystery and I advise you put a few hours aside and read this in one seating just don't forget to breathe!!" **Ellen Devenport - Bibliophile Book Club**

"Pressure is a fast paced thriller which is genuinely terrifying." **Joanne Robertson - My Chestnut Reading Tree**

"Betsy Reavley has gone and smashed it with her newest book Pressure, pure unadulterated tension which will intensify the fire within your imagination." **Diane Hogg - Sweet Little Book Blog**

"This is a great, fast paced and claustrophobic story that will keep you on the edge of your seat." **Jessica Bronder - JBronder Book Reviews**

"An addictive, compelling read that pushed me well out of my comfort zone - if you like disturbingly twisty plot lines and dark characters then this is definitely the read for you." **Lisa Hall, Author of the best selling psychological thriller Between You and Me**

"The Optician's Wife is a stylish, brilliantly crafted thriller which really delivers. A very real sense of creeping dread, combined with intelligent, finely drawn characters, had me turning the pages late into the night. This one will linger with you, long after the book is finished. Reavley has delivered a masterclass and deserves to be up there with the best in the business." **L J Ross - Bestselling author of The DCI Ryan books.**

"I love discovering new authors especially one who can shock and surprise me like this as it doesn't happen very often!" **Joanne Robertson - My Chestnut Reading Tree**

"Don't you just love it when you pick up a book and it blows you away, well Betsy Reavley has managed to do just that with a book that's absolutely filled with suspense and intrigue." **Lorraine Rugman - The Book Review Cafe**

"This was a fantastic book and one I knew from the first chapter it was going to keep me enthralled reading it." **Leona - Goodreads Reviewer**

"Wow! What a stunning book. Draws you in, spins you a line and boom! you've got it completely wrong. Loved it. So clever." **MetLineReader - Goodreads Reviewer**

"This is a book that once you start reading it you won't be able to stop. It is a story that grabs you right from the very beginning." **Joseph Calleja, Relax and Read book Reviews**

"This is true stand-out in the domestic noir genre." **Caroline Matson, Confessions of a Reading Addict**

"Betsy Reavley has reached new heights with this breathtaking book. Child abduction is always a difficult subject and she has totally embraced it in this outstanding book. It will leave you feeling emotionally drained and in awe of this author. Her best book yet, a literary masterpiece" **Anita Waller, best-selling author of 34 Days, Angel and Beautiful**

"Absolutely incredible book, cannot praise it enough. I think it's my best read of 2016." **Emma De Oliveira, an ARC reviewer**

"It went from heart pounding moments to adrenaline rushes where I simply couldn't speak. This is one of my top three books of the year, awesome!" **Susan Hampson - Books From Dusk Till Dawn**

"Reavley has written a stunning thriller which is fast-paced and full of twists and turns. I was completely invested in this narrative, submerged by the tension and gravity of the situation." **Clair Boor - Have Books Will Read**

For all my ladies. You know who you are.

"Nothing is impossible to a determined woman."

Louisa May Alcott

*"There are two motives for reading a book:
one, that you enjoy it; the other, that you can
boast about it."*

Bertrand Russell

If you're going to play with fire, you're going to get burnt – Proverb

Prologue

7.30am 22 June

It didn't take the Border Collie long to discover the source of the scent it had followed for the last five minutes. In amongst the red campion flowers lay a woman's discarded shoe. The dog sniffed eagerly, its tail announcing its excitement at the find.

From the path its owner whistled impatiently, waiting for the normally obedient dog to return, but Flo the collie didn't much feel like obeying orders today. The scent she had lucked upon was far more exciting and, nostrils flaring, she followed her large black nose deeper into the undergrowth. Her owner worried the dog was about to roll in a cowpat, left by the cattle that roamed the common every summer.

'Flo! Flo!' The woman, jogging on the spot, keen to get on with her run, called the dog repeatedly. When it became apparent that the dog was not listening to her, she stopped jogging and stomped towards the undergrowth, cursing to herself.

Standing in the low morning light, it was difficult to see much in the woodland on Stourbridge Common. A low mist hung over everything and the place was strangely still.

'Flo?' The woman spun on her heels when she heard the crack of a twig to her right, but the dog was nowhere to be seen.

Gingerly, the woman stepped deeper into the trees, being careful not to snag her Lycra running leggings on anything, but more aware of the damage that could be done to her ludicrously expensive trainers.

Her heart was beating hard and sweat sprinkled her brow as she pushed her way further into the thicket. She stopped for a moment to listen and could hear barking in the distance. Following the sound, she went deeper into the woodland, suddenly feeling very alone.

Through the mist she could make out Flo's tail wagging furiously, making the mist particles dance around like fairy dust.

'What the hell do you think you're doing?' The woman ranted, relieved to have found her dog but frustrated by her behaviour. The collie still wouldn't come to her, so she found herself clambering over wild shrubs to reach her.

Flo sat patiently, and waited for her owner to come and join in the discovery.

There, in the clearing, was a woman's body. Her hair was a mess and she was lying on her front, quite still, among the small red flowers. She was naked and bruised, and her head was caved in like an eggshell.

The woman stumbled backwards in horror and tripped over a large log, landing on the ground with a thud and cutting open the palm of her hand on a rock, as she let out a bloodcurdling scream.

CHAPTER 1

5.25pm 21 June

As Toni stepped out of her immaculate home onto the pristine lawn, she tucked her phone into her fake Gucci bag and smiled to herself. She stroked the side of the faux leather designer handbag with her nails – long, manicured and painted beige – and trotted away from the red brick bungalow, across the lawn.

Her curled, highlighted hair bounced with enthusiasm as she pulled her large sunglasses down over her deep brown eyes. She smelt good, she looked good and she knew it.

Above her, the clouds began to gather, shutting out the summer sunlight and casting a grey shadow over her world. But, as she wandered along the pavement, Toni seemed oblivious to the dip in the weather. Nothing was going to spoil her mood.

It was Thursday, and her favourite night of the week. Every Thursday evening, at 6pm, she met with the ladies from her book club. They chatted about the book they had all been reading, whined about their dull husbands, ate cake, and put the world to rights over a few glasses of Chardonnay. The evening felt no different to any other as Toni made her way towards Marion's house, looking forward to the next couple of hours.

Toni and her husband's bungalow was on a residential street to the east of Cambridge, just off Newmarket Road. Number 9, Ditton Way, was a small red brick, 1950s dwelling that was well kept. Toni's husband, Gerald, was a keen gardener. Toni joked that it was the only thing he was good at.

The couple had met online five years previously, after Toni's first marriage to Mike had collapsed.

Gerald was everything Mike wasn't: reliable, trustworthy, hardworking, and dull. Toni secretly wished that her marriage to Mike had worked out, but his alcohol problem became too much for her to cope with and she left him; the only blessing was that they'd never had children.

In Gerald she'd found a companion, one who could be compared to a lapdog. He doted on Toni, which she encouraged. Not only was he ten years her senior, he had never been married and therefore had no baggage, which appealed to Toni who liked to be in control of every aspect of her life.

As she crossed the road she felt the phone in her bag vibrate. When she reached the other side of the quiet street she checked the message.

See you soon sweets xx

The message was from Shirley, her friend and fellow book club attendee, who she would be seeing very soon at Marion's house, on the other side of town in Cherry Hinton.

Toni responded with two kisses before dropping her phone back into her bag and smiling to herself, trying to ignore her new heels that were rubbing against her ankles.

As she walked towards the bus stop, Toni had the feeling she was being followed. It was still broad daylight, so she dismissed the strange notion and waited patiently beneath the bus shelter for the number 5 to show up.

When an elderly woman pulling a purple floral trolley-bag came and joined her, Toni felt much better, despite the fact she couldn't shift the uncomfortable feeling of being watched.

The old woman, who had more facial hair around her chin than most men in their forties, sat down heavily on the bench and grunted as she searched for something in the compartment of her trolley-bag.

Toni, not much liking the smell of the elderly woman, took a step away from her and turned her head, craning to see if the bus was about to appear from around the corner. She made a mental note to let the old woman get on the bus first, so she could be sure she would not end up sitting anywhere near her. Toni had no time for people who didn't take care of themselves, and she prided herself on her own neat appearance. In some ways, it mattered greatly what other people thought of her, but she was known locally as someone who spoke her mind and she often ended up ruffling a few feathers. She was a woman who was sure of herself and thought herself to be above other people; she never questioned how she spoke to others, or conducted herself, much to the dismay of anyone who happened to be in her path.

As the bus appeared, Toni took a step back and signalled for the elderly woman to get on first. She was unable to do this without a look of disgust on her face, which made her look ugly, and the woman shook her head as she waddled towards the steps and onto the bus.

While she searched for her pensioners bus pass, the woman felt saddened by the look she had received from this stranger; she felt she had been judged without good cause. Yes, she was old and she had let herself go, but her husband of sixty-four years had died only six months ago, and she saw no reason why she should pretend to be happy.

When the elderly lady had finally taken a seat near the front of the bus, Toni threw some change at the driver without looking at him, retrieved her ticket and made her way upstairs, putting as much space between her and the woman downstairs as possible.

Adjusting her sunglasses, despite the gloom outside, Toni stared out of the window at the streets and people below.

As the bus took her towards the south-eastern side of the city, Toni felt herself tense. She hated it when it was Marion's turn to host, because Marion had a more prestigious address than she did: she lived in Cherry Hinton on Gladstone Way.

Marion, whose husband Alfred was an accountant at one of the largest firms in Cambridge, was a sweet natured woman who simply loved reading. She didn't care about her postcode or worry about buying expensive clothes. What Marion loved most was her husband, two children, her West Highland terrier called Josh, and, of course, reading. She was the opposite of Toni, who used the book club as a way of making friends and a name for herself.

When her marriage to Mike fell apart Toni was lonely, and turned to her computer for company. She went on numerous dating websites and soon became embroiled in an online book group. But Toni was frustrated by the group being online only, and took it upon herself to arrange a local book club that met regularly. She liked the idea of meeting new people and looked forward to finding some purpose in her lonely life. The book club had been going for two years and had grown from the original three members, of which Toni was one, to over fifteen – all women. Initially, men were invited to join – Toni had hoped she might meet her next husband through the group – but it became apparent that it would be best for it to remain a women only club, and so it was.

That Thursday, ten of the women were expected to be there. It was fairly normal that not everyone could make it every week, but Toni, without fail, was there each week.

The women took turns at hosting the club in their homes, and much to Toni's irritation it was Marion's turn once again. The only thing that made her feel a bit better, was the fact that Marion was twenty years her senior, grey-haired, and broad around the stomach.

When Toni knew her stop was coming up, she removed a small compact from her bag and checked her make-up. Her large, pale pink lips glistened with gloss as she kissed them together.

Getting off the bus in heels would have been problematic for most, but Toni had been doing it for years and had mastered the art with finesse. Gliding away down the street, she straightened her red top, making sure her bosom looked as pert as possible, and checked that her skin-tight white trousers were still spotless.

As she reached Gladstone Way, she plastered a smile across her face, ready for battle, and made her way up to the white front door of Number 33.

The detached house belonging to Marion and Alfred Bolton had a lovely front garden that was bursting with roses. Toni found herself inhaling the scent as the door opened and Marion welcomed her with a smile.

'Toni, good to see you, pet,' she beamed, stepping back and allowing Toni inside. 'How've you been?'

Marion was a Yorkshire lass born and bred, but had moved down from Harrogate to Hertfordshire when her husband Alfred was offered a job with a highly regarded accounting firm. The couple had two grown-up sons, one of whom was in the army; the other had married a Norfolk girl and moved to Norwich with his new bride to be closer to her family.

'Oh, you know, busy, busy.' Toni wandered through the hallway, past the kitchen and into the lounge, as if she was right at home.

On a large teak coffee table sat a tray of biscuits, a sponge cake and a pot of tea. The cake looked home-made and Toni made a mental note to brush up on her baking skills, ready for the next time she hosted the club. She was not going to be outdone by an old trout like Marion.

'Would you like a slice?' Marion picked up the knife when she saw Toni looking at the cake.

'Oh no. Not good for my figure.' She perched on the edge of the large M&S sofa and watched as Marion cut herself a huge slice.

'You're missing out,' Marion said, winking as she sank her teeth into the buttery sponge. Toni felt her stomach rumble.

'No sign of any of the others yet?' Toni struggled to hide her frustration.

'Don't look like it.' Marion shrugged, putting the slice of cake on a floral china plate while looking up at the clock on the wall. 'You're early,' she commented, brushing some crumbs off her trousers.

'I prefer the term "prompt",' Toni said through a sarcastic grin.

The two of them sat in silence, with only the sound of the ticking clock for company, until five minutes and forty-seven seconds later when Marion's doorbell chimed.

Quick as a flash, Marion was out of the armchair and dashing towards the front door. Alone in the room, Toni quickly hoovered up some of the cake crumbs that lay on the plate and sucked her fingers clean.

In the next room she could hear Marion welcoming Kim.

Kim had always lived in Hertfordshire. She'd married a builder, Pete, who ran his own business, and they had twin daughters and one young son. Kim and her family lived on the very outskirts of Cambridge in an area called Chesterton, to the north-east of the town.

Kim and Toni had known each other for some time, and met when Toni worked temporarily as the receptionist at DW Fitness First. Kim had joined the gym soon after having her twins, telling herself that she'd get fit and lose her pregnancy belly. In reality, Kim was more at home in a cocktail bar than at the gym, so it wasn't long before she had stopped her monthly subscription. The two women became friends after Toni had spotted a copy of a bestseller, that she was also reading, sticking out of Kim's sports bag. The pair fell into a conversation about books and they were both pleased to have found a fellow reader who shared their passion. Soon after that, they arranged to go for coffee and had been friends ever since.

Despite this, though, Toni had never approved of Kim. Kim was outspoken, loud, and loved a good party. Toni didn't like to drink and couldn't understand why anyone would. She also found that Kim often dominated the conversation, when Toni felt she should be the centre of everything.

Standing up to greet her friend, Toni made sure she hooked the fake Gucci bag over her arm so it would be seen. Much to her irritation, Kim owned a real designer bag, although Kim never felt the need to flaunt it in the same way Toni did.

'Darlin'!' Kim came bounding into the room and spread her arms wide, squeezing Toni in a tight embrace and planting a kiss on her cheek, which made her feel uncomfortable. Toni had never been good at dealing with people who invaded her personal space. Kim pulled away and pinkie-purple marks from her bright lipstick remained on Toni's cheek.

Marion had to hide a smirk as she returned to the front door after hearing a loud knock. Knowing there was only one person who refused to use the doorbell, Marion opened the door looking forward to seeing the familiar face of her friend Barbara.

'How've you been, chick?' Kim flopped down on the sofa, sitting very close to Toni in anticipation of further arrivals. 'I'm shattered. The girls are drivin' me mental!' She cackled, throwing her head back, showing all of her big white teeth.

'Yes, I'm fine.' Toni straightened her back.

'Look,' Kim said, reaching into her white leather Moschino handbag, 'I brought supplies!' Kim brandished the bottle of rosé high in the air triumphantly. 'Time to get this party started.' Kim unscrewed the cap and took a long swig as Toni folded her arms across her heaving chest and rolled her eyes.

Marion let Barbara in, giving her a warm hug.

'Good to see you,' Marion said, accepting a bunch of roses from Barbara.

'You too. These are from my garden. I know how much you love roses.'

'I do,' Marion said, pushing her nose into the arrangement and inhaling the scent up her rather large nostrils, 'how thoughtful.'

'You're looking well,' Barbara said, smiling at how well her present had been received.

'I only saw you last week,' Marion chuckled, leading Barbara into her living room to join the others.

Barbara's round face was rather red, and she fanned herself as she took a seat on the sofa opposite Toni and Kim.

'Nice to see you, ladies,' she said as a large bead of sweat dribbled down her temple.

'You too!' Kim said, sitting forward and putting the bottle of wine on the coffee table next to the cake, tea and biscuits.

'Subtle as ever,' Marion said, smiling and winking at Kim. 'How many glasses?'

'Not for me,' Toni said as she slid along the sofa, putting as much space as she could between herself and Kim.

'Me neither,' Barbara added, still fanning herself with her chubby hand.

'Just one then!' Marion turned and went towards the kitchen, leaving the other three sitting in an uncomfortable silence.

'How's things, Babs?' Kim asked while rummaging in her handbag for something.

'Very well, thank you. How are you and your brood?' Barbara was still slightly out of breath.

'Bloody nightmare! The girls are driving me to drink.' Kim chuckled as she held up the bottle of wine.

'You are wicked,' Babs smirked, wiping some more sweat from her brow.

'Right.' Kim stood decisively. 'I'm nipping out for a ciggie.'

Toni turned in horror, just as Kim slipped a cigarette between her lipstick-coated lips.

'You're smoking again?' She recoiled with disgust.

'I've tried those electric cigarette things, but nothing beats the real thing. A girl has to have her vices,' Kim said over her shoulder, as she slid the French doors open and stepped out onto the patio.

'Revolting habit.' Toni got up, shaking her head, and pulled the doors closed shutting Kim and the cigarette smoke outside.

'She's got a lot on her plate,' Barbara said, eyeballing the cake on the coffee table.

'No excuse!' Toni spat.

'You don't have children, do you?' Barbara said softly.

'No, I don't, and I'm grateful for that fact every single day. Neither do you, Babs.'

Barbara thought about saying something else but decided against it and instead stood, groaning as she did so.

'I'm going to powder my nose,' she said, leaving the room – and Toni alone.

Toni watched as Kim sucked hard on her cigarette while the silver smoke danced in a halo around her head. *She's certainly no angel*, Toni thought to herself, as she inspected with interest the outfit that Kim was wearing.

Kim had on an emerald green vest top and a white, ankle length gypsy skirt. On her feet were flat silver sandals and her wrists were adorned with jangling bangles. Her dark hair, with its bleached tips, sat on her shoulders and her fringe made her look young and carefree. She had a slender figure, which Toni envied.

When Kim noticed Toni staring she waved in an exaggerated manner, to which Toni turned her head and pretended not to notice. Kim wondered how Toni treated her enemies if this was how she behaved with her friends. As she took the final drag from her cigarette, she shrugged her shoulders and decided to forget it. Toni had been passive aggressive ever since she'd known her, and that wasn't suddenly about to change, but Kim did wonder, for a brief moment, why she put up with Toni's behaviour. She certainly wouldn't stand for it from anyone else. But she smiled at her old friend as she slid open the doors and stepped back into the house, just as the doorbell rang.

'I can smell it from here.' Toni pinched her nose with her fingers.

'I've got a couple of tampons in my bag. You can use them to plug yourself up, if you like?' Kim's eyes met Toni's and did not waver. At that moment Shirley came into the room, putting an end to the tension, closely followed by Janet.

'Alright, girls?' Kim said, flopping back onto the sofa.

'Yes, thanks,' Shirley replied, letting the cotton tote bag slip off her shoulder and fall to the floor. 'Sorry we're late. Someone wasn't at home when I got there to pick them up!' Shirley pointed a chubby finger at Janet, who hid a little laugh behind her long, thin, bony hand.

Marion returned and handed the wine glass over to Kim while offering everyone else tea.

'Can I join you?' Shirley grinned, showing off a mouthful of perfectly straight, large white teeth.

'I'll get you a glass.' Marion pretended to roll her eyes. 'Tea for the rest of you?'

Everyone nodded, and Marion returned to the kitchen to get on with making a pot of tea.

'I'm glad we're not the last ones,' Shirley said, blowing her dyed red fringe off her face. Her cheeks were flushed and she appeared more flustered than normal.

'Everything OK, chick?' Kim asked.

'Yes. Just hot.' Shirley smiled warmly. 'The weather is really close, isn't it?'

'They say a storm is coming,' Kim added.

'Something else to look forward to then,' Toni mused.

'What do you mean by that?' Kim bit back.

'Oh, nothing. Really, you are so sensitive sometimes.'

'I—' Kim began, but Marion appeared just in time to put a stop to the minor dispute, preventing it from escalating.

'Play nice, you two,' she said in a low voice, as she placed the steaming hot teapot on a coaster on the coffee table and handed over two wine glasses to Kim.

The room fell quiet. Marion had always been able to shut down any trouble within the group. People liked her and respected her, and they listened to her opinion. She was the unnamed mother of the club.

'Tut, tut,' Marion said, looking down at her gold wristwatch, 'they *are* late.'

'Shall we start without them?' Janet spoke with a slight lisp, which made any word she said sound like a gentle whistle. Her long, pale fingers gripped the designated book so tightly that her knuckles were white. She looked twitchy and unsettled, balancing on the arm of the sofa where Shirley was sitting, sinking into the pile of cushions.

'Yes. Let's.' Marion took up her position in a beige chenille reclining armchair. 'So, who wants to begin?' she asked, as Kim unscrewed the cap on the wine bottle and poured two very generous glasses.

'Chin-chin,' Kim said, smiling sarcastically at Toni, who turned her head away and put her nose in the air.

'So,' Marion sighed, shaking her head a little, 'I'll begin then.' She leant forward and saw Kim give Shirley a little wink before they clinked glasses.

'I liked it; I didn't love it, but I liked it. I thought the main character was good, and well-rounded, but something in the plot was missing for me. Maybe I found it a bit slow.' Marion fixed Toni with a stare, making sure she remained involved in the conversation. 'It reminded me a bit of *Possession*, by A. S. Byatt, but not as good. Have any of you read it?'

'Yes.' Kim lurched forward with excitement, almost spilling her wine on Marion's cream carpet. 'Yes, *Possession* was a great book. So well written.'

At times, Kim's enthusiasm was catching; at other times, it was purely irritating. She had a way of dominating the conversation that left others feeling elbowed out; this was one of the issues that Toni had with Kim. They both liked being the centre of attention and were both large personalities. Sometimes they got on like a house on fire, other times they didn't. It was always difficult for the rest of the group to know what to expect from one meeting to the next. More often than not, it all hung on the mood Toni was in, and today she was not taking any prisoners. Marion wondered if everything was all right at home, with Gerald. She rarely mentioned him, and Marion thought it was odd. Especially since they had only got married recently.

'Yes, I read *Possession* and thought it was very beautiful,' Janet joined in, her little piggy eyes sparkling with excitement. The only time Janet ever looked alive was when she was talking about books, or talking to Shirley. They were an odd pair, and you wouldn't have expected them to be friends. Toni had always questioned why Shirley was friends with Janet – Janet was a dowdy, rude and aloof person; Shirley was a lot of things, but she had a good enough brain and a great sense of humour. She wondered what Shirley got out of the friendship, and why she was happy to spend so much time with the miserable sod.

'I tried to read it, but it was too heavy for me,' Shirley piped up. 'I like easy reads, you know? I don't want to be bogged down with language and description. I get it was nicely written, but books like that just don't do it for me.'

Barbara, who wasn't really concentrating on the conversation, sat staring out at the garden, looking at the summer rain as it began to fall. Toni watched Barbara gazing at the rain, and wondered why the woman looked so sad. She was normally a jolly sort and it was obvious to Toni that something was wrong. She made a note to herself to corner Barbara before she left, so she could find out what was bothering her. Toni hated not knowing what was going on.

'Well, I for one would kill to be able to write like Byatt!' Marion clapped her hands together as the doorbell rang again.

'Better late than never,' Kim chuckled, glugging back her wine.

'They'll be drenched,' Barbara mused.

'Back in a tick.' Marion got up from her armchair and went to answer the door, leaving the room silent once again.

'You look like a drowned rat.' Toni smirked as Pauline, sodden, came into the room.

'Nice to see you again, Toni.' Pauline shook her blonde hair, which was normally as dry as straw, and went to give Janet a hug. Kim had to swallow her laughter. Although Toni had been rude, she did have a point.

'Can I get you a towel, pet?' Marion put her hand on Pauline's shoulder, before quickly removing it, wiping the dampness off her fingers and onto her trousers.

'Oh, yes, that would be good.' Pauline smiled, showing a mouthful of yellowing crooked teeth, as the frizz returned to her shoulder-length hair. At a guess, the other people in the group would have said she was in her late fifties, but no one really knew. She kept her age to herself – for reasons the other women greatly enjoyed speculating about.

Her cerise linen jacket was soaked through and sticking to her bulky shoulders; the white floral, knee-length dress had mostly been protected from the downpour. As Pauline tried to shake off the jacket, her large, flabby arms wobbled like jelly. On her feet she wore a pair of sandals, which were clearly too small as they cut into the flesh around her ankles.

'Right, what have I missed?' she beamed, unaware of the atmosphere in the room.

'Kim was just telling everyone how intellectual she is because she's read, and enjoyed, *Possession*, by A. S. Byatt,' Toni sneered.

'Oh.' Pauline's round cheeks flushed pink and her grey eyes dropped to the floor, not knowing where to look.

'My friend, ladies!' Kim held up her glass in a mock toast to Toni, and proceeded to drain it, much to the disgust of both Janet and Toni.

'Stop it!' Marion barked. 'You are meant to be friends. This is a book club, not a cat fight.' Her brown eyes were angry and she stared at Kim and Toni with contempt. 'This is my house and I won't have it. I'm telling you that for nothing.' Her thick Yorkshire accent bounced off the walls of her living room.

Pauline remained hovering, not sure where to sit – or even if she should. It was unlike her. Normally Pauline was extremely sure of herself and commanded the room. She was a tall woman, with a square jaw and an infamous stubborn streak. Seeing her thrown off-kilter like this was pleasing to some of the group, particularly Kim, who had taken a dislike to her the very first time they met nearly nine months ago.

Pauline had, at one time, been a manager at the local WH Smith on Market Street and, as a result, thought she knew more about the book world than anyone else on the planet. This irritated just about everyone in the group except Barbara, who took everything in her stride, and was not easily wound up by anyone except Geoff, her husband, who had died six years earlier. Despite *him* often irritating her, she missed him every day and he had been the love of her life. Now her life was quiet and empty, apart from the company of her two rescue cats, and the book club once a week.

In between meetings though, the women would often chat via Facebook. Barbara in particular relied heavily on the social media platform to fill her days. The book club had its own group page, of which sixteen women were members, although the core consisted of ten women, nine of whom were due at Marion's house that day.

On the group page, the women would post pictures of the books they were reading, leave reviews for the others to see, and fill the page with other bits and pieces that were loosely connected to anything bookish.

'Well, I for one am enjoying myself.' Kim leant forward to clink glasses with Shirley, who looked sheepish and refused. 'What's wrong with you all? You're all so boring!' Kim reached for the bottle of wine and topped up her glass.

'Leave then,' Toni sneered. 'I don't know why you bother to come.'

'Ha!' Kim threw back her head. 'I come because I love winding you up!' Janet stifled a laugh and Marion threw her a glance that said, watch it.

'Oh, fuck it.' Kim got to her feet and slammed her wine glass on the coffee table. 'I'm out of here.'

Barbara, who was looking distressed by the whole situation, put her hand up to her mouth. She couldn't abide bad language or confrontation.

'I think that might be best.' Marion stood and led Kim out of the living room, leaving the rest of the group stunned into silence.

'Well. That went off with a bang.' Shirley's eyes twinkled with joy.

'She's a mess.' Toni ran her hand through her hair and tried to look unflustered. 'She needs to get a hold of herself.'

'Those poor kids,' Janet whistled through her nicotine-stained teeth.

'You can hardly talk!' Toni curled her lip.

'What does that mean?' Janet hissed.

'Living in that grotty flat, above the bookies. Your kid doesn't ever see his father. You probably don't even know who his father is!'

The room fell silent as Janet got to her feet. Her skinny, hunched frame was shaking, and Shirley held out a hand to offer her friend some support.

'Well, at least I have a kid. No one would be daft enough to get you pregnant.' Her small, pale eyes were in thin slits and she spat as she spoke.

At that moment, the women were briefly distracted from their argument when they heard raised voices coming from the hallway.

'This meeting,' Toni said, standing up and gripping her handbag, 'is over.'

But before she had a chance to storm out, Marion appeared with Amy and Maggie.

'What have we missed?' Maggie smiled, entering the room, but as soon as she acknowledged the atmosphere her mood changed.

'What's happened?' Amy asked, her face pale and her green eyes wide.

Chapter 2

1.40pm 22 June

Barbara sat in her favourite armchair and put on the local lunchtime news. Bramble, her scraggy looking moggy, jumped onto her lap and made itself at home.

On the small table next to her, was a cup of tea and a cheese sandwich. It was the same thing Barbara ate for lunch every single day; she was a creature of habit. Occasionally, if she were feeling naughty, she would collect the crumbs of cheese on her plate and feed them to the cat, who was ever hopeful for the treat.

Outside her small council house her other cat, Rosebud, sat sunning herself on the windowsill. She was by far the more independent of the two felines.

After the summer storms of the past few days, the weather had cleared up and Cambridge was drenched in warm June sunshine, which Barbara welcomed. She hadn't been able to sleep well due to the humidity, and was relieved that the air was now lighter and the temperature more bearable.

Reaching for the remote control, she turned on the television in anticipation of watching the news and getting the latest weather report. On the screen, a pointy-nosed redhead appeared, sitting with her back straight, looking down the lens.

'Good afternoon. Welcome to Anglia News. These are the headlines: police have confirmed that the body of a woman was discovered in the early hours of this morning, on Stourbridge Common in Cambridge. The death is being treated as suspicious and the victim has not been named. A forensic tent has been erected and police have cordoned off the area. In other news ...'

'How awful,' Barbara muttered to herself, as she took a large mouthful of her sandwich and dropped bits of grated cheese onto her lap, which Bramble leaped upon with glee and gobbled up the titbits while purring with pleasure.

As quickly as the news of the murder entered Barbara's consciousness, it disappeared. She became quickly absorbed in the next story about library closures in the region.

'Terrible,' she said, shaking her head. The sound of the phone ringing in the hall distracted her from her lunch and she sprang out of her chair, displacing the cat, who glared at her with hatred as she hurried out of the room.

'Hello?' Barbara answered, brushing crumbs off her ample chest.

'Hello, pet.' Marion's voice travelled down the line.

'Marion.' Barbara was pleased to hear from her friend, 'I was just having a spot of lunch.'

'Did you see the lunchtime news?' Marion asked, already knowing the answer to her question.

'Oh, yes. Terrible about the libraries, isn't it?' Barbara tutted.

'Never mind that,' Marion huffed down the phone. 'Did you see about the body on the common?'

'Oh, yes, that.' Barbara felt her cheeks going red.

'Who would have thought,' Marion continued, 'in a nice, safe place like this. You just wouldn't expect it.' There was a silence, and Barbara wondered why Marion had really called her.

'Is everything alright?'

'Well.' There was another long pause. 'Have you spoken to any of the book group since the meeting on Thursday?'

Barbara racked her brains. Since Geoff had died, all her days seemed to merge into each other.

'No, I don't think so.'

'Well I have.' Marion sounded strange. Her voice was distant. 'Kim didn't go home after she left my house.'

Barbara let the information sink in.

'I've had Pete on the phone. He's worried sick.'

'Oh, dear.' It took a few seconds for Barbara to realise what Marion was hinting at. 'You don't think …'

'I don't know. I'm worried sick. Then the news today ...' Her words trailed off.

'I'm sure it's just a coincidence, love.' Barbara felt her blood run cold.

'Well I'm not hanging around here to find out. I'm going down there.'

'Where? To the common?'

'Aye. I can't just wait around hoping to hear some news. It's playing havoc with my nerves.'

There was another silence while Barbara decided what she was going to do.

'Let me finish my lunch and I'll come with you.'

'Are you sure, pet?' The relief in Marion's voice was tangible.

'I'm not having you go there on your own.'

'Oh, thank you. I'm not sure I could face it alone.'

'Give me ten minutes to leave the house. I'll meet you by the entrance to the common, at Water Street, in an hour. Although I doubt we'll get anywhere. The police aren't likely to talk to us two.'

'I have to try.' Marion's resolve was unwavering.

'OK. See you soon, love.'

'Ta. See you there.' Marion hung up, leaving Barbara standing in her hallway holding the phone to her ear for a moment longer than necessary. She didn't believe for a minute that the body on the common was that of Kim, but she could tell how upset her friend was and if it would help to put her mind at rest, the trip out would be worth it.

Barbara put down the phone and went back into her living room to discover that Bramble had pushed her plate off the side table and was greedily tucking in to her cheese sandwich.

With her hands on her wide hips she shook her head and rolled her eyes.

'Whatever am I going to do with you?'

Half an hour later, Barbara had filled up the cats' water bowl and made sure the windows were secure and the house was locked.

Stepping out into the June sunshine, she was pleasantly surprised when a warm breeze wafted down her street.

Barbara lived at Number 15, Nuns Way, close to Campkin Road, on the northern side of the city. The area was rundown and infamous for the gangs that congregated on the streets. She and Geoff had lived there for many years and while he was alive she'd always felt safe, but as old age was beginning to set in, Barbara no longer felt so confident walking through the streets. The youths were often sitting in their cars, with their engines running and music blaring. It made her feel uneasy, and that sunny Friday afternoon was no different.

She felt the beads of sweat gather at the nape of her neck when she passed a group of young Asian boys, who were all talking loudly, swearing, and smoking something she didn't recognise as tobacco. Barbara didn't think of herself as someone who was prejudiced, but she couldn't help feeling nervous as she went by, her head down, looking at the pavement. Of course, none of the boys did or said anything, but her pace quickened until she was sure she was far enough away from them.

By the time she arrived at the bus stop on Arbury Road, she was hot and breathless. Standing beneath the shelter, in the piddling amount of shade it offered, she tried to fan herself with her clammy hand. When she caught sight of the gold wedding ring on her finger she felt a pang of sadness. They had told her it would get easier, but the pain of losing her husband was still very much alive.

Thankfully, it didn't take long for the Stagecoach bus to show up. She got her bus pass out of her worn beige handbag and flashed it at the driver before taking her seat. She was grateful that there were some benefits to getting old.

Fifteen minutes later the bus stopped outside Cambridge North railway station. From there, it was a twenty-minute walk to the edge of Stourbridge Common, where the women had agreed to meet at the Water Street entrance.

Barbara felt stiffness in her knees as she climbed down off the bus, and made a mental note to buy some cod liver oil tablets on her way home.

As she approached the entrance to the common, she saw two policemen standing on either side of the pathway. Realising she wouldn't be permitted entry, she waited on the other side of the road for Marion to appear. Thankfully, trees lined the busy road and Barbara found a nice spot in the shade where she could sit and wait for her friend.

It wasn't long before she recognised Marion's stumping frame coming along the pavement; she walked with determination and surprising speed, Barbara thought.

'Looks like we can't go in,' Barbara said as she got up to greet Marion.

'Well it doesn't stop me going and chatting to those policemen,' Marion said, checking for cars as she marched across the road.

'Good afternoon.' The shorter of the two policemen nodded.

'Hello.' Marion suddenly appeared lost for words.

'Can I help you?' he encouraged.

'Well err, I saw on the news …'

The policeman rolled his eyes and looked at Barbara, who stood in silence.

'This is a new investigation and I am not at liberty to say anything about an ongoing case.' The officer was clearly enjoying his small moment of power.

'But my friend is missing.' Marion sounded choked and Barbara put her arm around her shoulder.

'Has this been reported?' The other officer stepped forward, suddenly taking an interest.

'I think so,' Marion continued, 'her husband is worried sick. She's got little 'uns.'

'The best thing you can do is go home, ladies.' The tall policeman sounded gentle and less harsh than his short, balding counterpart.

'I know it's her. I just know it.' Marion began to sob.

'Come on, love.' Barbara tried to lead her away, but she wouldn't budge.

'I have to know. You understand,' she pleaded, searching the kind policeman's face.

'As of yet, the body has not been identified and if, or when it is, the next of kin will be informed.' He shrugged, unnerved by the sobbing pensioner standing in front of him.

Marion nodded and let her head drop to her chest.

'Let's go and get you a cup of tea.' Barbara smiled sadly at the officers as she led Marion away down the road. 'I'll even treat you to a nice bun.'

Once seated in the café on Chesterton Road High Street, the ladies silently sipped their tea. The place was noisy with teenagers who had just come out of school and she wished they had chosen somewhere else.

'Geoff and I used to come here for breakfast on a Saturday.' Barbara finally broke the silence.

'I know how much you still miss him,' Marion said, putting her tea on the table with a trembling hand.

With a sigh and a nod, Barbara leant forward.

'Why didn't you tell me about Kim?'

'I don't know.' Marion shrugged. 'I thought it wasn't my business. I didn't want to be accused of gossiping.'

'It is odd, I must admit.' Barbara was looking down at the currant bun that sat in front of her, and she turned it around on the plate while she thought. 'She wouldn't leave her babies without saying anything.'

'Exactly. That's exactly what I keep thinking, which is why …' Marion didn't finish her sentence.

'You're jumping to conclusions, love. No good adding two and two and coming up with five.'

'Well, some poor woman is lying dead on the common. What am I supposed to think?'

'Have you spoken to Toni?'

'No. Not since book club.' Barbara watched as Marion stiffened.

'Maybe you should give her a call.'

'After the nasty things she said to Kim? I don't have any desire to speak to that woman again.'

'You've not been online much since the meeting.'

'No, I haven't. Because, in all honesty, I'm fuming. I can't believe them all, behaving like that when they were guests in my house. But now, what with Kim missing, well it just don't bear thinking about.'

'When was the last time you spoke to Pete?' Barbara picked at her bun and put a morsel in her mouth.

'This time yesterday, and then when I saw the news, I wanted to call him, I really did, but I just couldn't.'

'She might be back by now. If you call at least you'll know, one way or the other.'

'I'm not sure my nerves can hack it, Babs.' Marion shook her head and pushed her cup of tea away. To Barbara, she appeared five years older and tired.

'But even if she isn't at home, it doesn't mean the person in the woods is her.'

'No, agreed. But it doesn't look good. I've been on this planet too long to believe in coincidences, pet.'

Forty minutes later they were back at Barbara's house. She'd insisted that Marion came home with her since Alfred was out for the day playing golf, and she didn't want Marion at home, alone, worrying about Kim.

While Marion sat in the living room, Barbara excused herself and went to make a phone call. She felt silly interfering, but she needed to speak to Pete for herself. The call lasted approximately ninety seconds.

'She's home!' Babs burst into her living room clapping her hands together. 'She's back!'

'Who? Kim? Oh, thank goodness.' Marion's shoulders dropped and she slumped into the sofa, suddenly overcome by exhaustion.

'Pete said she went to visit her friend after leaving your place. He didn't half sound angry. Apparently, she came home with her tail between her legs just after lunch. Seems she was cross when she left your place, after all that business with Toni, so she went to her friend Gina's house, and the two of them ended up in a pub. Kim lost her mobile and when she got back to Gina's place she was too drunk to call home.'

'That silly girl!' Marion couldn't decide if she was relieved or livid. In truth, she felt a bit of both.

'She's safe and sound and that's what matters,' Barbara stated, putting the conversation to bed.

'I don't half feel daft now,' Marion admitted.

'You're a good friend. You were just worried.'

'I'm a silly old woman.'

'Don't be so hard on yourself, love.' Barbara patted her friend's shoulder. 'It's frightening when someone is killed so close to where you live. Not surprising you were thinking all sorts. Unnerving, is what it is.'

'Aye,' Marion said wistfully. 'Well, it's a relief knowing Kim is safe, but all that means is some other poor family can expect a call from the police sometime soon.'

Chapter 3

4.40pm 22 June

Gerald was in the shed when he heard the distant sound of the doorbell. He rubbed his hands on his jeans, wiping earth from them, as he made his way across the small semi-paved garden and into the house.

'Just coming,' he grumbled, as a loud knock shook the white plastic rim of the front door.

Standing on the other side were two suited men. Around their necks hung lanyards. Both looked solemn and official.

'Can I help you?' Gerald asked, clearing his throat. The smell of earth still tickled his nostrils.

'Mr Gerald Jones?'

'Yes.' Gerald felt the blood drain from his face. This wasn't good. Whatever *this* was.

'I'm DCI Barrett and this is DI Palmer. Can we please come in for a moment, sir?'

'Why?'

'It's a sensitive matter, sir. It would be much better if we went inside.' DI Palmer, who hadn't spoken, didn't look Gerald in the eye. He peered out into the street, looking at anyone who stopped to be nosy, warning them off with his cold stare.

'Yes.' Gerald stepped back, letting the officers into the small house and closing the door behind them. 'Go through into there,' he gestured with a shaking dirty hand.

The small, badly lit, but clean, living room was hot and stuffy.

'We think you should take a seat, sir,' DCI Barrett continued. Gerald did as he was told, his balding head glistening with sweat.

'What's going on?'

'We are here about your wife, sir. Is your wife Mrs Toni Jones?' DI Palmer stood stiffly in a corner, looking at the ornaments on the mantelpiece.

'What about her?' Gerald's voice quivered.

'We have reason to believe …'

'Oh God.' Gerald put his round head in his hands and let out a moan.

'Sir,' Palmer said as he moved closer and spoke in soothing tones, 'when did you last see your wife?'

Gerald looked up into Palmer's deep blue eyes, searching for answers.

'Yesterday. She left to go to her book club.'

'What time was that?' Barrett took a step forward, wanting to regain control of the interview. Palmer, knowing his place, moved back to let his superior do his job.

'Why are you asking me these questions?' Gerald looked small and fragile sitting in the chair. Palmer and Barrett both found it difficult to imagine him being married to the victim.

'We have recovered …' it was Barrett's turn to clear his throat, 'a body.'

'No.' Gerald's steely grey eyes filled with anger and he stood. 'Impossible. She is with a friend. That's all. You'll see. She just decided to stay with a friend. I'll call her now. I'll prove it.' He reached into his pocket and removed his mobile phone. Before he was able to summon her number, Barrett's hand came down and clenched his wrist.

'I am afraid we will need to seize your phone.'

'What?' Gerald glared at the DCI suspiciously.

'A body was discovered on Stourbridge Common this morning. We have reason to believe that the victim is your wife.' Barrett swallowed, and loosened his grip a little. 'I am sorry.'

Both men, who were now standing, locked eyes. Barrett's gaze did not waver, but Gerald crumpled into a heap on the orange and brown 1970s carpet, his whole body shaking.

The policemen looked at each other, not sure what they should do. For Palmer, this was the first time he'd had to break the news of a murder to a relative. Barrett was much more used to this part of the job, but had never seen a reaction like Gerald's before.

'Get the man a glass of water,' Barrett barked to Palmer.

Palmer, pleased to be leaving the room, skipped off to find the kitchen. He was grateful to be away from the heavy atmosphere, if only for a moment.

'We are going to need you to come to the station with us.' Barrett squatted on his heel so he could be face to face with the man who was falling apart in front of him. 'Is there anyone you'd like us to call?'

'How do you know it's her?' Gerald managed to croak.

'We found a handbag containing her driving licence at the scene.'

Gerald looked past the detective and out through the net curtain as if he'd noticed something. Barrett followed his gaze but saw nothing.

'Sir?'

'She might have just lost her handbag. Or had it stolen.' Gerald appeared pathetic, but Barrett understood the man's need to clutch at straws.

'The photo ID, well …' he hated this part, 'it matches the appearance of the deceased.'

Gerald sat in the back of the car looking blankly out of the window. It didn't take too long to drive through the city to Parkside police station in the centre. Once the car had pulled in, and the officers had got out, they opened the door for Gerald and encouraged him out of the car. He was on autopilot and did as he was told.

Once inside the tall grey building that overlooked Parker's Piece, Gerald was led to a room and offered a cup of tea, which he declined. It wasn't tea that he needed, it was Toni.

'I understand this is a very difficult time for you, Mr Jones, but I'm afraid we need to take a statement.' DI Palmer sat on the plastic chair opposite Gerald and crossed his legs.

'I want to see her.' Gerald straightened up, trying to look taller and more confident than he was.

'I'm afraid I wouldn't advise that at the moment.'

'What do you mean by that?' Gerald's piggy eyes filled with tears.

'Your wife was brutally attacked.'

'No!' Gerald let out a low moan and buried his face in the palms of his hands.

'I know this is difficult, but we need to ask you some questions.'

Gerald lifted his face; snot was running from his nose, over his lips and down his chin.

'We need to know where you were last night.' DCI Barrett removed a tissue from the box on the table and handed it to Gerald.

'I was at home.'

'Can anyone corroborate that?'

'I was alone.' Palmer and Barrett threw each other a knowing look.

'Can you tell us what you were doing?'

'I was watching telly.'

'What did you watch?'

'A show about gardening.'

'What time was that?'

'Oh, err …' Gerald looked decidedly flustered, 'I think … maybe eight o'clock.'

'You think?' Barrett leant in closer, studying the man's face. 'This is a murder investigation, sir. The details are important.'

'Don't talk to me like I'm an idiot. I am an upstanding member of my community.' Gerald's cheeks flushed red with anger.

Barrett sat back in his chair, cocked his head slightly, and lifted the end of his navy tie, pretending to pick something off it. It was clear that Gerald was unnerved by the silence and he wriggled in his plastic seat, making it creak loudly.

'I can prove I was at home,' he said. Palmer looked at Barrett and raised an eyebrow. 'My car …' he tripped over his words, 'it was damaged. A fire engine ran into it. They tracked me down to my home using the registration number. I think one of them was called Steve. He and his colleague knocked on my door to let me know what had happened and to apologise. They were on a call and it was a mistake. The road was narrower than they realised, and they were obviously travelling at speed. I told them not to worry but they insisted on taking all my details and said that their insurance would cover it.' Gerald's broad smile was triumphant. 'There,' he said.

'What time was that?'

'I don't know when they hit my car, but the knock on the door was around nine-thirty.'

'What make is your car?'

'It's a Renault Clio. Forest green colour.'

'Right. Well we will check your story.' Barrett looked slightly irritated. There was something about this man that he didn't like or trust. One minute he was playing the distraught widower, the next he was acting smug. 'Moving on. Can you think of anyone who might want to harm your wife? Did she have any enemies?'

Gerald looked down at his grubby fingernails and thought for a moment.

'No. Not that I'm aware of.' His response was too aloof for Barrett's liking. 'Perhaps I will have that tea after all.'

Barrett nodded at Palmer who got up and left the room.

'What was your last conversation with your wife about?'

Gerald swallowed hard and shifted in his seat again.

'Well, we …' his eyes refused to meet the detective's, 'we had a bit of an argument.'

'I see.' Barrett's bright blue eyes sparkled. He loved the hunt. 'Can you tell me why you were arguing?'

'Oh, it wasn't very serious. She was just cross that I had spent the day in the garden and not with her. But in this weather, you have to take extra special care of the plants. Despite the heat, I spent a lot of the day in the greenhouse tending to my tomatoes and things.'

'I see.' Barrett didn't believe Gerald's story.

'The last thing she said to me was that I was a waste of space.' His face fell, and he appeared more dejected than any other man Barrett had ever come across. He found himself suddenly pitying his suspect.

'Okay, Mr Jones. I think that will do for now. I'd be grateful if you could pass on the details of the book club Mrs Jones was attending, to DI Palmer. I also have to warn you that we will need to collect some of your wife's possessions from your home. Her computer, and any other items we deem relevant to the investigation, will be seized. We will do everything in our power to bring her killer to justice, but it is important you cooperate fully with our investigation. Do you understand?'

'Yes.' Gerald began to sob again.

'You will be allocated a Family Liaison Officer who will keep you informed of all our enquiries. In the meantime, is there someone you would like me to call?'

Gerald's wet eyes searched the room looking for an answer that seemed to elude him.

'I suppose we should call her sister.'

'I'm going to need a number,' Barrett said, as Palmer appeared, carrying a polystyrene cup of steaming hot tea.

'It's on my mobile phone. Her name is Hilary. Hilary Newton. She lives in London.'

'Are there any other members of the family who need to be informed?'

Palmer was pleased to put the hot tea on the table and he shook his hand to relieve his fingertips.

'No. Her parents are both dead.' Gerald paused again for a moment. 'She has an ex-husband.' The officers glanced at one another. 'I suppose he might want to know.'

'Did she have any children with her previous husband? We'll need his name.' Barrett's pen was poised, ready to capture the information.

'Mike Williams. He lives in Great Shelford with his new wife, Amber, and their young daughter, Lucy.'

'Thank you, Mr Jones. The information you have given us is very useful.' Barrett drew a large circle around Mike's name before getting up to shake Gerald's hand as DI Palmer led him out of the room.

Barrett looked at the notes he'd taken. He would be following up the details regarding the firemen, and cursed that Gerald appeared to have an alibi. There was something about the man that Barrett found suspicious, although he couldn't put his finger on it yet.

Walking down the corridor, he thought about the home that Toni and Gerald had shared; there was something staged about it, something that didn't sit right. He tried to remember what it was that had caught his eye on the mantelpiece, and suddenly remembered it was the wedding photo of Gerald and Toni. There was nothing particularly unusual about the picture, except that the groom was beaming, and the bride looked distracted. In the photograph, Gerald had his eyes glued on his new bride, and Toni was looking at something else out of shot. Something about her expression troubled Barrett – he'd thought she looked angry – and it struck him as odd that they would chose that picture to display in the house as a memory of their special day.

There was something odd about their marriage, Barrett knew it. Now all he had to do was work out what it was, and discover if it was linked to her murder.

Opening the doors to the investigation room, Barrett was greeted by a flurry of activity.

'Chief Inspector?' a female colleague called and waved at him from her desk, while holding a phone to her ear. 'I think you are going to want to hear this.'

Chapter 4

7.25pm 22 June

Gerald felt drained; he still couldn't absorb what had happened. Without seeing her, it didn't feel real. Perhaps they had made a mistake. He knew the police were checking Toni's dental records and that it would be confirmed, or not, in a short amount of time.

Back at his house, he sat helplessly on the sofa while police officers combed the house for anything they thought would help with their investigation. He couldn't ignore the fact that they were certain it was Toni they had found in the woods. His head was pounding and the world was beginning to spin, so he took himself into the bedroom he once shared with his wife.

Light was streaming in through the net curtain, making a floral pattern on the floor. On the wall, opposite the bed, stood Toni's dressing table. He went and sat where she had sat the previous morning. He'd always liked to watch her do her make-up, even though she found it irritating: 'Go and do something useful', she would snap, as she rubbed the thick orange-brown foundation into her pitted skin. As always, Gerald would do as he was told.

With a sigh, he picked up her perfume bottle and held his nose to the nozzle. He closed his eyes and pictured his wife as she flounced out of the garden, leaving a trail of her scent behind her, after saying some vicious things to him. That was the last time he'd seen her alive.

He had built a life for himself and found a purpose when he married Toni. Now he wondered what lay ahead for him. With his brain whirling around, Gerald got up from the dressing table and lay down on their marital bed. He lay on Toni's side with his face buried into her pillow. It was warm from the sunlight pouring into the room, and he managed to convince himself, for just a second, that she had been lying there only moments before.

Tears came streaming down his face making the pillow wet, and he hugged his knees up to his chest as he let his emotions flow. Gerald was not a man used to crying, and the action itself caused additional upset.

When he could cry no more he lay on the bed staring at the wallpaper. It was pink and white with a small floral pattern. Toni had chosen it when she moved in. She said the place needed a woman's touch, and Gerald had let her do as she pleased.

The couple had met via an online dating site when her marriage to Mike had fallen apart. Gerald remembered the first time he met her as if it were yesterday.

After a few weeks of emails, and talking on the phone, they had agreed to meet at the entrance to the Cambridge University Botanic Garden. Gerald had been very nervous, as his experience with women up until then had been limited. He wore a brand new shirt that he'd bought for the occasion from M&S, and even put on a splash of cologne. Balding, and in his early fifties, he was conscious that he might be a disappointment to Toni – even though they had exchanged pictures and seen one another's profile online.

He had stood anxiously outside the gates to the garden, awaiting her arrival with fear and anticipation. Gerald always liked to be early, and was taken aback when she too arrived five minutes earlier than the time they had agreed. His hand was clammy as he'd awkwardly shaken hers; he thought she was beautiful. Her long, thick hair had glistened in the low light and her make-up was expertly applied.

As they had wandered slowly around the grounds, he was increasingly aware of her height. With her heels on, she was at least two inches taller than him, so he'd walked with his back straight, and his head held high, in an attempt to lessen the difference. On that warm, spring afternoon she'd worn the same perfume she always did. It was sickly-sweet, like vanilla and violets. Toni had worn a white dress that hugged her curves, a light blue cardigan, and wedge shoes.

She had spoken endlessly about her first husband and the break-up of their marriage. Gerald listened carefully as she recounted stories about the times Mike had been drunk and difficult to live with. Gerald had felt such pity for her. She didn't deserve the treatment she had received, and he for one knew he would never treat any woman like that.

Their first date lasted a little over an hour, and Gerald had left knowing that Toni was the woman for him – even if he wasn't sure she felt quite the same.

Their meetings continued, and things progressed at a speed he had not been prepared for. She was a woman with a keen sex drive – for which Gerald was extremely grateful. He'd not had many girlfriends and did not share the experience of his new companion, but he was certainly a very willing pupil.

Gerald had always been a mortgage advisor. He worked at a mortgage brokers in Teversham – a slightly rundown village that had been swallowed by Cambridge many years ago. His father had worked as a broker before him and Gerald had never had any expectations that he would do anything different. The Mortgage Solution Centre was on a quiet industrial road, behind Cambridge Airport. For most people, it would have been a depressing place to work, but Gerald never seemed to notice.

At the time, Toni was working as a receptionist at the DW Fitness First gym, located in the Beehive Centre, an industrial estate just off Newmarket Road. She was older than the other people on the desk, and clearly hated the job, but following the collapse of her marriage, she had to do something to put a roof over her head. They had been renting a house, but Toni could not afford to keep it on after Mike had moved out. To Gerald's horror, he discovered she was living in a bedsit in Trumpington, a residential area on the southern outskirts of the city.

The bedsit was in a building that looked more like a concentration camp than a block of flats, and the place itself was riddled with damp, which made it smell of mould and used to make Gerald sneeze. He felt dirty when they stayed there, and it didn't take him long to invite her to live with him. Much to his surprise she had jumped at the opportunity. Within twelve hours of their engagement she had quit her job. He felt like a man who had just won the lottery.

When they were together in public the couple would receive many looks. Gerald told himself it was because everyone was so enraptured by her beauty, but in reality, they made an odd pair. The age gap, as well as their height difference, made the couple stick out like a sore thumb, but Gerald was blind to strangers' sniggers: he only had eyes for Toni.

They met in early May and by October they'd married; it was a small civil ceremony that had taken place at Shire Hall, the council offices at the top of the only hill in the city.

Toni had worn a cream trouser-suit, and had her hair piled up on her head, the odd carefully placed ringlet escaping. Gerald had wanted to wear a brown suit he had in his wardrobe; but, after much persuading, he had gone shopping with Toni, who insisted that he wore a black suit with a pink shirt and tie. Despite not feeling comfortable in his clothes, it had been the happiest day of Gerald's rather dull life.

It didn't take Toni long to completely redecorate Gerald's soulless bungalow and turn it into a princess's palace. Apart from not replacing the carpet in the sitting room, which Toni had admitted didn't actually need replacing for anything other than aesthetic reasons, the entire place had received a makeover. The small dining room was turned from dull white to a deep, lipstick red. Their bedroom was a pink paradise – according to Toni – and their living room was decorated with a bold, lime green, patterned wallpaper that Toni had insisted Gerald liked.

After Toni had worked her magic on the bungalow she turned her attentions to Gerald, but soon found that orchestrating his transformation would not be anything like as easy. Despite not being the strongest character, Gerald was happy with who he was and didn't feel the need to change what he said, how he said it, what he wore, or what he ate.

A year after they had married, the relationship turned sour. Much to his disappointment, the boisterous sex dried up and Toni spent more and more time away from the house, enjoying the benefits of her husband's income. If Gerald had had any friends they would have been tempted to say something to one of them about his new wife's behaviour, but he had always been a solitary man. That was, until he met Toni.

Now, lying on the bed with his head resting on a pillow soaked with his tears, Gerald struggled to see how his life could go on. He had lain there until darkness fell, and only moved when the phone next to the bed started ringing.

Sitting up slowly, he reached for the receiver without thinking.

'Hello?' His voice cracked.

'Gerald, is that you?'

'Speaking. Who's this?'

'It's Shirley.'

Gerald froze, it was Shirley from Toni's book club; he hoped she wouldn't ask to speak to his wife. He wasn't ready to deal with the outside world just yet.

'Is Toni there?'

'I ...' Gerald couldn't speak.

'Is everything alright, Gerry?' Shirley was the only person who ever called him that.

'I'm just on my way out. I'll speak to you soon.' He just managed to get all the words out before he slammed down the phone. The vultures were circling, he could sense it, and it left him feeling uneasy.

Leaving the dark bedroom, he returned to the living room where he found the Family Liaison Officer who had been assigned to the case, sitting in a chair reading a book. She looked up at him and offered a sympathetic smile.

'I thought perhaps you were sleeping.' She closed the book and put it on the table next to her, just like his wife would have done.

'No.' He felt parched and longed for a glass of water.

'Gerald, I have something to tell you. Forensics have been in touch and they have confirmed the body on the common is that of your wife. I am truly sorry.' She stood and watched him as he sat down slowly on the small, white, faux leather sofa.

'She's gone then.' His eyes were wide and fixed on the picture of them on their wedding day.

'I'm afraid so.' The officer put her hand on his back. She could feel his shirt was damp with sweat and he could feel the heat radiating from her palm.

'What am I going to do with myself now?' Gerald turned to face her and searched her hazel eyes, but found no answers.

This was the worst part of her job, and Julie could not wait to get home to her husband to hug him and their son tight.

Chapter 5

8.40am 23 June

After dealing with her six-year-old twin daughters, May and June, who were born hours apart as 31 May became 1 June, Kim waved them goodbye as they left for gym class with their father. She tidied the mess of breakfast plates and turned her attention to Dylan, her eighteen-month-old son.

'Who's going to be a good boy for Mummy today?' she said, reaching into a drawer and removing a packet of cigarettes, while Dylan sat in his highchair rubbing banana into the tray.

The chaotic kitchen had doors leading out to the garden, and, while Dylan was busy making a mess, she slipped out to have a cigarette, still keeping an eye on him.

It was colder that morning than it had been the past week, and she wished she had a cardigan for her shoulders. The sky was grey and still. It didn't look likely that the barbeque they had planned for lunch would go ahead.

Kim puffed furiously on her cigarette, wanting to make it back into the house in time to watch the morning news. She liked to keep abreast of what was going on in the world. She had an interest in people and politics and was an avid news follower.

At 8.50am she went back into the house and washed the smell of smoke off her hands before wiping down the highchair and removing Dylan from it. He toddled off purposefully in the direction of the living room and Kim, smiling, followed.

The living room floor was a mess of dolls and building blocks. Sweeping some out of the way with her foot, she went and sat down on the large grey sofa; she turned on the TV and went straight to the Sky News channel.

After sneering at the headline about Donald Trump's latest decision, she leant forward to pay careful attention. A young man wearing a suit was standing on a path that led through Stourbridge Common, and behind him was a forensic tent.

'Police have now confirmed the identity of the body discovered here yesterday morning. The victim, Antonia Jones, is a local woman. Her next of kin have been informed. Cambridgeshire Police were not willing to say any more at this stage, but have confirmed that they are conducting a murder inquiry. Back to John in the studio …'

Kim's mouth fell open and she reached for the remote so she could rewind the programme. She couldn't believe her ears and doubted that she'd heard right, but after listening to the report for a second time, she knew she had heard correctly.

Her hands shaking, she turned off the news and sat in silence for a while watching Dylan, who was pushing building blocks around aimlessly, before removing her mobile phone from her jeans pocket.

'Amy?' Kim could hear her voice shaking.

'Morning, woman!' Amy sounded jolly.

'Have you seen the news?'

'No. Why?'

'It's Toni. She's dead.'

There was a long silence before Amy responded.

'Don't joke. It's not funny,' Amy teased.

'Chick, I'm not joking. She's fuckin' dead. It's all over the news. The body on the common. It's Toni.'

The silence that hung between them was deafening.

'She can't be,' Amy stuttered.

'I know.' Kim suddenly had the urge for another cigarette and picked up Dylan with her free arm. 'It's fucked up.'

'What? How? I can't believe it.' Amy stumbled over her words, trying to process the information.

'They are sayin' it's murder,' Kim added gravely.

'But we only saw her on Thursday.'

'I know. It's mad.' Kim slipped Dylan back into his highchair as he started to whine and wriggle. 'We'd better let the others know.' Kim's head was spinning as the news started to sink in.

'Oh, Christ.'

'You know they'll want to talk to us.' Kim sounded nervous and breathless.

'Why? We were her friends. We saw her on Thursday night and they found the ...' she paused, wanting to find a nicer word, 'body on Friday morning.'

'Poor Gerald.'

'Yeah. Poor bloke. He'll be lost without her.'

'I know she and I didn't get on very well, but no one deserves this.'

'Shall we try and arrange a get together, with all the other book club ladies?' Kim put a cigarette between her lips and lifted the lighter to it with a quivering hand.

'It might be a good idea,' Amy added. 'We can do it here. My place is the most central and easiest for everyone to get to. I'll start to call round now and ring you back when we have something in place.'

'OK.' Kim's stomach felt empty and she knew it was nothing to do with the fact that she hadn't eaten breakfast. 'Sounds like a plan.'

'Are you OK?'

'I don't know, to be honest. It's a shock, isn't it?'

'Certainly is.' There was another silence. 'I'll call you back, OK?'

'OK. Speak in a bit.'

'Chat soon,' Amy said, hanging up the phone and looking around at her dishevelled bedroom.

Amy lived in a Victorian house on Mawson Road, just off Mill Road, a cosmopolitan street full of delis, cafés and restaurants, popular with students and families alike.

She had only recently moved into the house with her husband, Johnny, an architect who often spent time working away in London. She looked down at the small bump and stroked her belly; she was six months pregnant, expecting their first child.

Johnny had been in London for most of the week, overseeing a build for a huge development, and she wished for a moment that he was at home with her. She didn't know how to take the news of Toni's death; the two women hadn't got on very well, due to differing opinions. Suddenly, Amy felt alone and frightened – if Toni could be murdered on Stourbridge Common, surely it could happen to anyone? It didn't bear thinking about.

Amy got out of bed wearing Johnny's T-shirt, which she always wore when he was away, and went into the bathroom to splash some water on her face before looking at herself in the mirror. Despite feeling tired, her skin was glowing and she was thankful that the pregnancy had been kind to her so far. Scraping her hair into a messy bun, she drank a glass of water before returning to the comfort of her bed to make the phone calls she was dreading.

She sat, with the duvet pulled up around her waist, propped up against some pillows, looking at her mobile phone as if it were an alien piece of equipment. She couldn't decide who she should call first. She knew the order didn't really matter, but she wanted to handle the situation properly and with a sense of order. After some deliberation, she decided it would be Marion she spoke to first, since Marion had hosted the book club gathering on Thursday night, which was the last time any of them had seen Toni alive.

As she held the phone to her ear, waiting for Marion to answer, a lump formed in her throat.

'Hello?' Marion sounded far way.

'Marion, hi. It's Amy.'

'Oh, hello, pet.' The line crackled.

'Sorry, Marion, but it's not a very good line.'

'Hang on, I'm just in the garage looking for something. I'll move into the house. One sec.'

Amy held the line – as well as her breath. How do you tell someone that their friend has died? Could Marion and Toni even be described as friends? Questions flitted around Amy's head as she waited to hear Marion's voice again.

'Is that better, pet?' Marion's words were now as clear as a bell.

'Much better.'

'What can I do for you?'

'Well, I don't really know how to say this, but something awful has happened.'

'Not the baby?' Marion gasped.

'No, no, not the baby. It's Toni. I've just spoken to Kim on the phone and, well, she's dead.'

'Oh, thank goodness!' The words left Marion's mouth before she had time to think. 'Oh, no, I didn't mean, I just meant, the baby, it's good, I'm glad it's okay. Oh my ...' Her flustered words rushed down the line.

'Maybe you should sit down,' Amy suggested gently. 'It's an awful shock, I know, I only heard myself a short while ago.'

'Never mind me,' Marion huffed, 'are you sitting down? Stress is no good for pregnant women.'

'I'm fine, Marion, honestly. I mean, it's awful, but Toni and I were never that close.'

'She was a difficult woman to get to know,' Marion mused, remembering her last meeting with Toni. 'So, do you know what happened?'

'What do you mean?'

'I mean, how did she die?'

'Oh ...' Amy paused, trying to find the words to break it to her gently. 'Well, she was murdered.'

'Murdered?!' Marion shouted. 'How? When? Oh my good lord.'

'They found her on Stourbridge Common on Friday morning,' Amy added, shuddering at the thought.

'The body on the common was Toni?' Her voice had gone up a note.

'It seems so. I don't know any more than that. Kim saw it on the news this morning. They've only just released the information.'

The line was quiet, and Amy wondered if Marion had fainted or something.

'Marion, are you there?'

'Yes, pet.' Her words were measured.

'I know there isn't anything any of us can do, but I think perhaps we should arranging a meeting with the other ladies from the book club. It's just awful news and we should all come together at this time. Don't you think?'

'That makes plenty of sense.' Marion sounded distant and clipped and Amy wondered if she'd said something wrong.

'Johnny is away in London on a build, so I was thinking of suggesting everyone came here this afternoon. I can nip to the bakers and pick up some cake. What do you think?'

'OK, pet. You do that. Is there anything I can do to help?'

'Obviously we need to let everyone know. Perhaps you could make a few of the calls?'

'Consider it done.' Marion had gone into organisational mode. 'What time shall I tell them to come to yours?'

'Half past three, or as close to that as they can manage. I know it's short notice.'

'Don't you worry about that. They will all be there, I'll make sure of it.' And Amy knew she would.

At precisely three twenty-five, there was a knock on Amy's red front door. She opened it to find Barbara and Marion standing on her doorstep; she gave them a small welcoming smile before letting them in, and led them through to her living room.

One wall was made up of nothing but shelves that were crammed with books. Marion, who had been to the house a number of times before, ran her fingers along the spines of some of the books. She knew Amy was a proper book lover, and not just someone who paid lip service in order to be part of the group for social reasons.

'Well, I never thought we'd find ourselves having to do this.' Barbara sat on the worn brown leather sofa and shook her head. 'I just can't believe it.'

'Hello!' Maggie appeared, carrying a tray that held a teapot and a large plate of cakes. She'd been at Amy's house for the last hour. As she bent to put it on the coffee table, her purple-rimmed glasses slipped down her nose. 'They look good, don't they?' she said, admiring the cakes while standing upright and pushing her glasses into place.

'They do,' Marion agreed, giving Maggie a welcoming hug.

'How are you?' Maggie asked, her tone more serious at last.

'I don't really know, pet. It's a shock, isn't it?'

'Yes, it is.'

Amy sat quietly in the corner, picking at a small hole in her leggings and twirling a strand of her hair round her fingers.

'You know,' Marion said, taking a seat next to Barbara, 'we were at the common yesterday. I was worried it was Kim.'

'Why?!' Amy looked horrified.

'Because she didn't go home after book club. Pete was awful worried. Then, when I heard she was home safe and sound, I didn't give much more thought to it. The murder I mean. Never did I think it could be anyone I knew.'

'Sends shivers up my spine.' Maggie wriggled on the spot to demonstrate her point and Amy had to disguise a smile. Maggie was known for being slightly over the top from time to time. 'Well, I'll tell you something for nothing: it's made me want to keep my kids in. Terry agrees with me. We don't want them wandering around while this stuff is going on. I told Jamie and Leigh, they aren't to be out when it's dark. I know they're teenagers and everything, but I put my foot down.' Amy and the others could well imagine how that had gone.

Terry, Maggie's husband, was a nice, quiet man who adored his wife. They'd been together for twenty years and had a solid marriage. He worked as a carpenter and she ran her own cake business from home. They lived in a large white semi-detached house, just off Arbury Road. 'I mean, you wouldn't let your kids walk around when there is some deranged killer on the loose, would you?' She spoke to Marion, who was struggling to get a word in edgeways.

'It's not right. I've been keeping my eye on the news and listening to the radio, but they aren't giving out many details. I think the local people have a right to know what's gone on.'

'The police will have their reasons,' Amy interrupted.

'I know,' Maggie carried on, waving a hand, the amethyst and diamond engagement ring on her finger catching the light, 'but they've told us nothing. Except that it was poor old Toni.'

'It's early days, I suppose,' Marion chipped in as the loud doorbell sounded.

'I'll get it.' Maggie sprang into action before Amy could get out of her seat. The three remaining women sat in the living room listening to Maggie greet whoever was at the door.

Seconds later, Shirley and Janet appeared. Janet looked as downtrodden as ever and Shirley smiled warmly.

'Alright, girls?' Shirley was wearing a lime green vest and black shorts. She looked like she belonged on the beach in Bognor Regis.

'Good, thank you.' Marion was always rather formal when talking to Shirley, for reasons the others didn't understand. 'How's Kayla?'

'Yeah, she's good thanks. A handful. Strong-willed, some would say,' Shirley chuckled, 'but she's occupied with her friends this weekend, so all is well.'

Kayla was Shirley's thirteen-year-old adopted daughter. She was spoilt, rude and unpleasant. The rest of the group dreaded it when Shirley hosted the book club, because Kayla would always be sure to play her music as loud as possible in her bedroom, which was directly above the sitting room where they gathered. She did not like it when her mother's attention was focused on anything other than her, and she made sure that everyone knew it. 'I dropped her in town so she could go and do some shopping while I came here. Can't believe *why* we are here. It's mad.'

'You know the police will want to talk to us all.' Janet's words whistled through the gap in her teeth as they always did. It was the first thing she had said since arriving. 'We all saw her before she died so they'll want statements.'

'Didn't know you knew anything about how the police work?' Maggie said suspiciously.

'I know a lot of things,' Janet snapped back, plunging her hands into the pockets of her long, beige, cable-knit cardigan.

'A lot about nothing,' Maggie muttered under her breath, just loud enough for Amy to hear. It was the second time in less than five minutes that she'd had to stifle a grin.

'I heard they found her naked,' Shirley cut in.

'Really?' Maggie looked shocked. 'Where did you hear that?'

'Oh, one of Grant's friends works at Addenbrookes, where they've taken the body. He heard it from someone, apparently.'

Grant was Shirley's husband.

'You don't have to look like you're enjoying yourself so much, you know?' Amy folded her arms across her chest.

'Oh, shut up. I'm just telling you what I heard.' Shirley looked briefly embarrassed before her expression turned to anger.

'She was a proud woman. I hope that isn't true,' Barbara said thoughtfully.

'But she did like being the centre of attention,' Maggie added. 'She is certainly that now.'

The room went quiet. It was true, but no one had been brave enough to say it. Maggie, who had never really seen eye-to-eye with Toni, had only said what everyone else was thinking – even if it was a bit inappropriate.

'What? She wouldn't have held back, would she, if it had been one of us?'

'Well, that's true,' Marion agreed.

'It's not like we are all best friends. She was a pain in the arse,' Amy said. 'It wouldn't be right to pretend otherwise just because she's dead.'

'Is that what you'll be saying to the police?' Janet asked sarcastically.

'I won't be lying.' Amy's expression was measured. 'Why, will you? Will you pretend you liked her, Janet, just like you did when she was alive?'

'Shut your face, Amy. Leave her alone. You walk around acting all perfect, like butter wouldn't melt, but you're just a bitch,' Shirley pitched in.

'Pot and kettle,' Amy laughed.

'What does that mean?' Shirley's face flushed red.

'You and your little friend,' Amy jabbed her finger towards Janet, 'you pretended you liked her. We all know what you really thought. You told us all enough times! But you wanted to join the book group and you knew the only way in was to make friends with her. You're pathetic.'

Shirley and Janet shared a look.

'Oh, what, cat caught your tongue? I've got messages from you calling her every name under the sun. Deny it all you like, but you're full of it. The pair of you.'

'I don't remember you being very complimentary,' Shirley spat back.

'No. I didn't like her, but I didn't pretend to. She knew perfectly well what I thought about her. I didn't hide it. We worked out a way of being in the same room without having to be fake.'

'I'm not fake,' Shirley and Janet said in tandem.

'You're as fake as the nails that Toni used to wear!' spluttered Maggie, coming to Amy's defence.

'I'm not your friend and I won't pretend I am. Let's just be clear that I don't care about your Instagram pictures of your bloody house or your ugly kid. You do my head in. Your insincerity makes me sick.' Amy's words silenced the room.

Marion got to her feet.

'I'm sick of this. We were all meant to be coming together so we could discuss this like adults. You lot are worse than school children. A woman has been murdered, close to where we all live, and to make matters worse we all knew her. You're all so wrapped up in the past you can't see what's right in front of your bloody noses. I'm not listening to any more of this. I'm going home. Stay here and fight, for all I care. Sod the lot of you.'

Marion looked at Barbara, who followed suit and stood up.

'I'm going too,' she said sheepishly.

'I thought you were better than this, Amy.' Marion shook her head with disappointment as she left the room, closely followed by Barbara.

'Well, I'm not hanging around to be insulted.' Janet wiped the back of her crooked, dripping nose with the back of her hand.

'You know where the front door is.' Amy sat in her chair, pretending to inspect her nails.

Shirley and Janet both marched out without saying a word.

'Well, that went well,' Maggie chuckled.

'I'm sick of it.' Amy finally felt able to show her anger. 'I've bitten my tongue for long enough. It's toxic and it isn't good for any of us. I've been thinking about it for a while, but now I've made up my mind. I'm leaving the book club.'

Chapter 6

3.30pm 23 June

DCI Barrett and DI Palmer sat in silence as they drove towards Great Shelford. Each had their wild theories about the murder of Toni Jones, but, as yet, no real motive had presented itself.

As they travelled along the High Street, it didn't take them long to find Mike Williams' cottage, which was in a picturesque spot next to the Square and Compasses pub.

Parking the silver Volvo S60 on the pavement, Palmer and Barrett got out of the car and approached the front door of Number 21. From inside, they could hear the cries of a toddler having a tantrum and both were dreading the door being opened.

It only took a moment for an attractive blonde woman to open the door. She was smiling but, when they held up their badges and introduced themselves, the smile quickly melted from her face.

'You'd better come in,' she said, stepping back; her white sundress ruffled from the breeze that followed the detectives into the cottage. 'Mike,' she called upstairs to her husband, who was clearly the one battling the toddler.

'He'll be down in a minute,' she explained, tucking a strand of her smooth blonde hair behind her ear. 'Can I offer you something to drink?'

'I'd take a glass of water,' Palmer said.

'Not for me, thank you, Mrs Williams,' Barrett added.

'Oh, please, call me Amber.' Her dark brown eyes were smiling at him and for a moment Barrett thought he might get lost in them. 'It's absolutely shocking news about Toni,' she continued, showing the policemen through into the small but cosy lounge, as the toddler let out another bloodcurdling scream.

'Sorry about Lucy. She's teething at the moment and it's making her very bad tempered.'

'Mrs Williams,' Barrett said, opening his small notebook and ignoring her request that he should call her by her first name, 'can you tell me where you were on the night of June twenty-first?'

Amber's eyes widened and she looked startled.

'Why, yes, I was here, with Mike.'

'All evening?' Palmer asked.

'Yes. All evening.'

'And neither of you went out at all?'

'No, well, I went to get some milk but—'

'What time was that?' Barrett interrupted without any embarrassment.

'Oh, maybe seven, or half past. Something like that. It was before we ate dinner. I'm pretty sure of that.'

'And what did you have for dinner?' Barrett continued, refusing to alter his line of questioning.

'Thursday night, I think we had baked potatoes and salad.' She tried to recall the meal.

'You think?'

'No, I'm certain. That's what we ate.'

'Gentlemen,' Mike announced himself as he came into the lounge. He was an exceptionally tall man with broad shoulders and a short beard. The cottage had low ceilings and he had to hunch slightly when coming through the doorway. In his arms was a young, red-faced little girl.

'Mr Williams. I'm DCI Barrett and this is DI Palmer. We are here to talk to you about the death of your ex-wife.'

'I thought you might be.' Mike handed his daughter to Amber and sat down, placing his hands on his knees.

'Your wife has told us you were both at home on the evening of June twenty-first. Is that correct?'

'It certainly is.'

'She says you had dinner together. Can you remember what you ate?'

'Salad and a baked potato. Washed down with a nice bottle of red, if I remember correctly.' Mike was steady in his response. Barrett took an instant dislike to the man, but told himself it was nothing to do with the fact that he was married to a very beautiful woman.

'I'd like to talk to you about Toni.' Barrett turned the page of his notebook. 'Can you tell me why your marriage ended?'

Mike looked over at Amber and the two shared a moment.

'Is that really relevant?'

'We are looking into the victim's life. You were a part of that for some time. I'd say that was relevant,' Barrett sniped.

'Very well,' Mike sighed and crossed his arms. 'She had an affair.'

Barrett raised an eyebrow.

'Can you be more specific?'

'She was fucking someone else.' Mike eyeballed the detective who squirmed a little.

'Who did she have an affair with?'

'I'd rather not say.' Mike clenched his jaw.

'Why not? This is a murder investigation. Withholding information is a serious offence.'

'Look, gentlemen, if you prove that her death is somehow linked to the affair, I'll spill the beans. Until then, I am not saying anything.' He was steely in his resolve.

'Very well.' Barrett adjusted his tie. 'When did you learn of the affair?'

'About three days before I walked out.'

'I'm going to get Lucy a drink.' Amber excused herself, wanting to put as much space between her body and the atmosphere as she could.

'I see.' It was Palmer and Barrett's turn to share a look. 'This is different to the information we've received.'

'Oh, let me guess!' Mike clapped his hands together loudly. 'You've been speaking to Gerald.' He said the name with obvious disdain. 'Gerald is a fool. He believed everything Toni told him.

She had him wrapped around her little finger. I almost felt sorry for the man.'

'Mr Jones told us that your marriage to Mrs Jones ended because of your addiction to alcohol. You claim this isn't true?'

'Of course it's bloody not!' Mike's voice grew louder. 'That's what she told him and those friends of hers, rather than admit she was a cheating bitch. It was a pack of lies.'

'Without giving us the name of the man you claim your ex-wife was having an affair with, it is very difficult for us to corroborate your story.'

'It's not a story,' Mike growled, 'it's the goddamn truth.'

'What did you make of that?' Palmer said, pulling the seatbelt across his body and fastening it before starting the car.

'Not sure.'

'Do you think he was telling the truth?'

'I didn't like him, but in all honesty, yes, I think that was the truth. At least his version of it.' Barrett looked down at the notes he'd jotted.

'We should talk to the husband again. Maybe he knew the truth and was covering for his wife.'

'So far, Joe,' Barrett undid the top button of his shirt, 'I think it appears that Gerald was completely blind when it came to his wife.' Despite calling the DI by his first name, Barrett insisted on being addressed as sir. He had rules in place and liked things just so.

'Where next, sir?' Palmer kept his eyes on the road.

'Back to the station. We need to do some digging. If the victim did have an affair when she was married to Mr Williams, I want to know who with.'

'Have we heard from forensics yet?' Barrett pulled his tie loose and placed the palms of his hands flat on his desk. The case, although in its very early stages, was beginning to irritate him. He'd wanted to have a suspect at the very least.

'Yes, sir,' a young, bright-eyed sergeant answered. She wore thick black-rimmed glasses and reddish-brown lipstick, although it didn't suit her mouth.

'They are placing the time of death around seven pm on the night of June twenty-first. The Home Office pathologist says she died as the result of blunt force trauma to the head. Whatever was used, hit her repeatedly.' The sergeant swallowed down the horror of the details. 'They believe perhaps a hammer was used, although, despite a detailed search of the murder scene, no weapon has been recovered. The killer, they believe, was right-handed.'

'Any sexual assault?' Palmer asked.

'No signs of sexual assault.'

'So why remove her clothes then?' Barrett pondered.

'There is something else.' The sergeant flicked through the file. 'Some petals were discovered in the victim's hair that could not have come from the scene.'

'Petals?' Palmer asked, looking incredulous.

'Yes. Red geranium petals. Horseshoe geranium to be exact. The pathologist says he believes they were planted on the victim.'

'What the hell?' Palmer scratched his head. This was most unusual.

'Carry on,' Barrett barked, wanting to know every detail.

'That's about it, sir.'

'I want you to find out everything you can about horseshoe geraniums. I want a report on my desk within the hour.'

'Already done, sir.' She flashed a smile at him. It still wasn't easy being a woman in the force. It remained very much a man's world.

'Horseshoe geraniums are native to southern Africa, but are grown in gardens across the country. You see them everywhere, sir. Even the supermarkets often have them for sale out the front in the spring. They are popular bedding and pot plants. They are called horseshoe because of the marking on the leaves. They come in a variety of colours and normally flower from March to June.'

'Anything else?' Barrett was beginning to get a headache.

'Yes, sir. I looked into the possible relevance of these particular flowers, and learnt that each flower has its own meaning. The geranium means stupidity or folly.'

'You think this was a message?' Palmer got up and reached for the pathologist's file, flicking through the photographs of the crime scene.

'It's certainly possible,' she said, nodding her head.

'The question is, Sergeant, is the message for the victim or for us?' The sergeant shrugged at that point and put down her notes.

'There is another possibility, sir,' Palmer spoke slowly.

'Don't say it, Joe.' Barrett shot him a look.

'Say what?' asked the sergeant, looking perplexed.

'Serial killer,' said Barrett quietly. 'Palmer is thinking this could be the start of something. But you never said it; you never thought it. If the press gets hold of this we'll have a media frenzy on our hands. It's too early to jump to any conclusions. Follow the evidence and let's keep to the facts, people.'

Chapter 7

3.50pm 23 June

'Sounds like I missed the fireworks.' Kim's eyes twinkled.

'You certainly did.' Maggie sat comfortably on the sofa, with her legs up, holding a plate that was home to a huge piece of chocolate cake.

'Well, it needed to be said. It's been going on like this for ages. Well done you.'

'I'm just surprised you weren't the first to say it!' Maggie wiped a smear of chocolate icing from her lips.

'Well, I kinda did on Thursday night. I feel bad now.'

'Oh yeah, we missed that. What exactly happened?' Maggie put the plate down, having devoured the cake.

'You know what she was like. She had a bee in her bonnet that day. Kept sniping at me and I wasn't in the mood. Everyone always put up with her shit, but I wasn't going to. I didn't get why she was being like that. It was odd, thinking about it.'

'In what way?' Amy asked, slowly stirring her tea.

'Dunno. It was like something was bothering her and she decided to take it out on me.'

The ladies sat contemplating what might have been worrying Toni.

'You do all know the truth about her and Mike?' Kim said in a half whisper, as if Toni was listening in the next room.

'No. What do you mean?' Maggie leant in and also spoke quietly, which was very unlike her.

'Toni was only having an affair.' Kim sat back, satisfied by the comment.

'No. You aren't serious?' Amy put down her tea.

'I am. Mike and Pete used to drink in the same pub, and Mike told Pete one night after a few. Never said who it was though. But he gave the impression it was someone he knew.'

'Wow.' Maggie shook her head. 'I don't believe it.'

'I didn't either. Mike is well fit. Why would she cheat on him?' Kim raised her shoulders and held out her hands.

'Poor Mike. I had no idea. I thought he was a drunk. That was what she told Marion.'

'Bollocks, all of it!' Kim picked up her glass of wine and sipped it thoughtfully. 'You know, now she's gone, I wonder if I ever really knew her.'

'I wonder if anyone did,' Amy said thoughtfully.

'What I did know I didn't like. I know you shouldn't speak ill of the dead and all that, but it's the truth. She rubbed people up the wrong way and had an ego the size of Russia.'

'Yeah, that's true,' Kim said, swishing the wine around in her glass, 'but she was the heart and soul of the book club. It will be weird without her.'

'I've had enough. I'm leaving it,' Amy added.

'Really, chick, why?'

'Two words: Shirley and Janet. I've had it up to here. I don't want to have to suck it up anymore. Toni's death has just brought it home to me. Life is too short. They're nasty people and I don't want to be around them.' Amy said this knowing very well that Kim and Shirley got on. 'I'm not asking anyone to pick sides, I know you like Shirl, but I just don't want to play that game anymore.'

'I didn't know she'd got under your skin so bad,' Kim admitted.

'It's a lot of things that have led to this. I don't know. I don't trust her, I don't like her, and I don't want to spend any more time in her company.'

'I think that's fair enough.' Maggie could always be relied upon to support her friend.

'You know,' Amy mused, 'the person I really don't want to upset is Marion. She's a kind soul and she'll be gutted to see the book club fall apart.'

'I suppose it's to be expected – when one of the group is murdered it's likely to put a strain on everything.' Maggie began to pour herself a cup of tea. She had refused the offer of a glass of wine from Kim, who was doing a good job of polishing off the bottle she'd brought with her on her own.

The other ladies nodded in agreement.

'But things were messed up before Toni was killed,' Kim added.

'That's true,' Maggie agreed. 'I know you'll think I'm daft for saying it, but I've wondered about that.' She paused and sipped her tea. 'Don't you think it's strange that she died when she did?' Maggie looked at the two women opposite her. They both waited for her to embellish. They knew she would, without any encouragement.

'Well, there was a big argument and she stormed off on Thursday. That's right, isn't it?' Kim nodded. 'And then she turns up dead. I'm just saying …' Maggie let the statement hang in the air.

'Come on, you don't really think they are linked?' Amy looked incredulous.

'I dunno. Someone killed her, didn't they?' Maggie shrugged.

'But surely not over some stupid argument at a book club meeting.' Amy got up and started to tidy things from the coffee table onto the tray.

'Murder at the book club. It kind of has a ring to it!' Kim chuckled. 'You do make me laugh, Mags.'

'Well, say what you will, but I don't believe in coincidences,' Maggie said huffily.

'It's probably some nutter.' Kim drained her glass and reached for the bottle.

'I hope you're right, because if you're not then it's someone we know, and the thought of that makes me feel sick.'

Amy stopped and stood up to rub her stomach. The baby was kicking.

'Can we change the subject, please?' she requested.

'Whatever you want, chick. I'm just pleased to be away from the kids for a bit, and Saturday day drinking is a definite bonus!'

Kim left a few hours later, slightly worse for wear.

'You don't really think someone at the book club killed Toni, do you?' Amy was in the kitchen preparing supper for her and Maggie. The onion she was slicing was irritating her eyes.

'Well, they say that people are most often killed by people they know.' Maggie sat at the kitchen table nursing a glass of Pinot Grigio.

'It doesn't bear thinking about.' Amy blinked back her tears, which were making it hard to see.

'Everyone has their secrets,' Maggie said, as she ran her finger around the rim of her glass.

'Oh yeah?' Amy chuckled. 'What's yours then?'

'I'm actually Superwoman.' Maggie winked.

'That's not a secret. I already knew that.' The onions sizzled as they hit the oil in the pan. 'Spag bol OK for dinner?'

'As long as there is garlic bread.'

'I got some in specially.'

'Great. You know me so well.'

'I'd kill for a glass of wine.' Amy looked longingly at Maggie's drink.

'You can have one or two every once in a while.'

'I know, but I feel guilty when I do.'

'Would you rather I didn't drink? I don't mind.' Maggie pushed the glass away.

'No reason we should both suffer.' Amy added mince to the pan.

'It didn't go very well today, did it?' Maggie fixed Amy with a stare.

'No, I don't suppose it did.'

'I wonder what will happen to the book club now.'

'I don't care. It stopped being fun some time ago. Toni's death just brought it all out in the open.'

'Shirl really is a cow.'

'I know. I can't believe she used to be my friend. What was I thinking?'

'You're trusting. You like to see the good in people.'

'Well, I'm certainly less trusting now.' Amy went over to the fridge and removed the bottle of white wine. 'I just don't get where it all went wrong,' she said, pouring herself a glass.

'I think I know.'

'Do tell?' Amy sipped the cold wine, savouring the taste.

'It was when you started writing. She didn't like it.'

'Why?'

'No idea, but that was when she started being bitchy.'

'She said she'd wanted to write a book but never actually started one. You did. I think that pissed her off.'

'That's insane.'

'Maybe so,' Maggie agreed, 'but that's when she changed.'

Amy shrugged and took another sip.

'How is the book coming along by the way?'

'Slowly. I'm caught up in research at the moment, which is slowing me down.'

'I can't wait to read it.'

'If I ever finish it!'

'You will. I have faith.'

'Can you believe what Kim said about Toni having an affair? What was she thinking?'

'I know. Kim kept that quiet!'

'I wonder if Gerald knows?'

'Doubt it. Probably wouldn't believe it anyway. He thought the sun shone out of her arse.'

'Well, if that's the case, I hope he never finds out. Let him look at the world with rose-tinted glasses. It doesn't matter now.'

Chapter 8

4.30pm 23 June

DCI Barrett and DI Palmer arrived outside Number 9, Ditton Way and Palmer killed the engine.

'Time to speak to Mr Jones again,' Barrett said, getting out of the car.

The men approached the bungalow and knocked on the door. Julie, the FLO, answered it.

'Hello, sir.' She stepped back, letting the detectives in. 'He's sitting at the kitchen table.'

When Barrett and Palmer went into the kitchen they found Gerald staring at a photograph of Toni that he was holding in his hand.

'Good afternoon.' Barrett cleared his throat, announcing their arrival.

Gerald looked up slowly, his face grey and his eyes red.

'We need to talk to you about Toni's first marriage.' Barrett sat on a chair opposite Gerald. 'We've spoken to Mike Williams, her first husband. He tells us that their marriage ended because Toni had an affair. Can you tell us anything more about this?'

'An affair?' Gerald looked perplexed. 'He had an alcohol problem. That's why she left.'

'No, Mr Williams has told us that he discovered she was having an affair and that was why the marriage ended.'

'Well, he's lying!'

'No, Mr Jones, I don't believe he is. I have to ask, were you the man in question?'

'I met Toni after their marriage had ended, she was divorced by the time we met. It wasn't me!' Gerald looked deeply offended.

'And you don't know who it might have been?' Palmer stood behind Barrett.

'No idea. This is the first I've heard of it.' Gerald put the photograph on the table, face down, and folded his arms. 'Do you think it is somehow linked to her death?'

'We are exploring all possibilities.' Barrett's frustration was tangible. 'Is there anyone who might know who Toni had an affair with?'

'Surely Mike knows,' Gerald said huffily.

'He doesn't want to tell us at this time.' Palmer stiffened.

'Maybe speak to Kim Geller? Those two were as thick as thieves for a while, and she would have been at the book club.' Palmer and Julie shared a look.

'Do you have an address?' Palmer removed a notebook from his trouser pocket.

'Yes, she lives on Lynfield Lane. Number 5, I think.'

'Thank you, Mr Jones.'

'I can't believe this is happening. It's all wrong. I want my wife back.' He put his head in his hands and began to sob. Julie approached and put her hand on his back.

'We'll leave you in peace,' Barrett said, leaving the room, closely followed by Palmer. 'I am very sorry for your loss.'

'You drive.' Barrett closed the front door behind him. 'We're going to Lynfield Lane.'

'Yes, sir.' Palmer took the keys from his pocket.

Ten minutes later they were north of the river, sitting outside Number 5, Lynfield Lane. The executive family house was in the Chesterton area of the city.

Barrett and Palmer approached the house and knocked on the door.

'Hello?' A tired looking man opened the door. 'Can I help you?'

'Good afternoon, I'm DCI Barrett and this is DI Palmer. We were hoping to speak to Kim Geller?'

'I'm Pete, her husband. She's not here.' A toddler appeared at his feet and tried to get out of the house.

'Can we come in, Mr Geller? We are investigating the murder of Toni Jones.'

'Alright then.' Pete scooped up the child and let the men in, guiding them into the living room, which was a mess of toys.

'Have a seat, gents.' Pete moved some building bricks off the sofa. 'I'm just going to check on my girls. They're playing in the garden. Back in a tick.'

Barrett sat awkwardly on the sofa, surrounded by the mess of everyday family life. Palmer could sense he felt uncomfortable and found it mildly amusing. His boss was a strange creature.

Pete reappeared and flopped down onto the other sofa, opposite Barrett.

'I'm shattered,' he admitted, wiping his brow. Barrett's face remained expressionless.

'Did you know Toni Jones?' Palmer asked, wanting to fill the silence.

'A bit. She was a friend of Kim's. She didn't come around much.'

'How long have they been friends?' Barrett held a pen poised above his notebook.

'They met about six years ago, I think. After the twins were born. Toni was working at the gym that Kim joined. That's how they got to know each other. Now they go to the same book club. Toni started it, I think.'

Meanwhile, Dylan, Kim and Pete's son, had come into the room and was bashing a toy drum loudly.

'I see.' Barrett scribbled something down.

'Why do you want to talk to Kim?' Pete sat forward, appearing slightly concerned. 'She was staying with a friend the night Toni was killed.'

'We want to talk to her about a delicate matter in Mrs Jones' past. We hope she might be able to shed some light on it.'

'Well, she's not here.' Pete sat back, looking more relaxed despite the increasing noise level coming from the toy drum.

'Do you know what time to expect her back?'

'Not the foggiest. She's a law unto herself, that woman.' Pete smiled.

'In that case, there is no reason for us to keep you.' Barrett stood up, eager to leave. 'This is my card. Please ask Mrs Geller to get in touch as soon as she can.'

'Will do.' Pete took the card and showed the men to the door.

'I think we need to interview everyone who was at that book club. I want a list of names.' Barrett sat in the passenger seat examining the notes he'd made earlier.

'Yes, sir,' Palmer said as he started the engine.

*

Sitting on a bench, opposite Parkside police station, Janet tucked in to a chocolate éclair she'd bought from the bakery cum coffee house on Mill Road.

Shirley sat beside her, still reeling from the argument at Amy's house.

'That bitch,' she hissed, as they sat in the warm sunshine.

'Better out than in,' Janet giggled.

'Who does she think she is? Talking to me like that. She needs to be taught a lesson.' Shirley's brown eyes sparkled at the thought.

'What are you going to do?' Janet wiped cream off her pointy chin.

'Dunno yet, but she's not going to get away with it.'

The pair sat in silence, enjoying the summer sun for a moment before Janet spoke.

'The police will probably want to talk to us.' Her words were slow and considered. 'What are you going to tell them?'

'What do you mean?' Shirley turned to Janet, looking somewhat alarmed.

'About where you were.'

'I was at home.'

'Was Grant there? Or Kayla?'

'No, he was out with the lads, watching the World Cup. Kayla was staying at a friend's house. Why? Where were you?'

Janet folded the paper bag that had contained her éclair.

'I was also at home. Alone.' Their eyes met for a moment.

'You really think they'll want to talk to us?' Shirley looked down at her large feet.

'I'm sure of it.'

'But we're just a book club.'

'We were the last people who may have seen her alive. Apart from her killer, that is.' Janet sniffed. Hay fever often troubled her. 'What do you think will happen to the book club now?'

'I dunno.' Shirley shrugged and wrapped her arms around herself as if she was cold.

'It won't be the same without Toni.'

'That's true. Maybe it will be better.' Shirley's words were filled with venom.

'Don't let the police catch you saying things like that,' Janet warned.

'You've got a point.'

Janet ran her hand through her thin, greasy hair and pulled it back into a ponytail. 'I was thinking, you know, just to make life easier, we could say that we were together after the book club.'

'OK,' Shirley agreed, without hesitation.

'You know, we don't want the police wasting their time by looking into us. That's all.'

'Good idea.' Shirley smiled. 'You're so thoughtful.'

'I'd do anything for you. You know that. No point wasting time on us middle-aged women.' Janet grinned.

'Less of the middle-aged, please!' Shirley nudged her friend in the arm and both women laughed.

'Do you want to come over to my place tonight? The chip van will be just down the road, I could get us some dinner.'

'Nah, not tonight. Can't. Got to get back.' Shirley checked her Fitbit, which was meant to encourage her to exercise but had achieved no such thing.

'Another time then.' Janet couldn't hide her disappointment. 'A quiet night in for me.'

'Where's Dean?' Shirley enquired after Janet's teenage son.

'He's always out these days.'

'How old is he now?'

'Nineteen.' Janet grimaced.

'I forget how grown up he is.'

'Not grown up enough to do his own washing, or take the bins out.' She rolled her eyes.

'You should find yourself a nice man,' Shirley encouraged, 'maybe join a dating site or something?'

'No,' Janet said as she wriggled on the bench, 'it's not really me.'

'I'm not saying you're lonely or anything,' Shirley backtracked.

'I know. I don't need anyone else though. I have you.' She rested her head on Shirley's round shoulder.

'Well, you know I'm always here.' Shirley patted her friend's head and then got up. 'Right. Time for me to go. Call, text or message me on Facebook later, if you like.'

'I'll do that.' Janet appeared very small, sitting on the bench alone.

'Alright, sweets. Speak soon.' Shirley waved over her shoulder and removed the car keys from her shorts pocket.

Janet watched as the distance between their bodies grew, and she felt utterly alone.

Chapter 9

6.30pm 23 June

The phone rang in the station room at Parkside police station and Sergeant Elly Hale picked it up. After listening to the officer, who was calling from the front desk, she spoke.

'Yes, patch it through.' She covered the mouthpiece with her hand and signalled to Palmer. 'Get the DCI. Kim Geller wants to talk to him.'

Palmer jumped up from his desk and knocked on his boss's door.

'Sir, Kim Geller is on the phone.' Barrett jumped to attention and shot off towards the sergeant who was still holding the phone.

'Mrs Geller. Thank you for getting in touch. I'm DCI Barrett and I'm in charge of the investigation into Toni Jones' murder.'

'Yes, hi. My husband told me you came to the house.'

'Indeed.' Barrett had the mental image of her little boy bashing his drum, and tried to push it out of his mind.

'I'd like to talk to you about the night Toni was murdered. We need some information. Would you mind if I came over with a colleague and took a statement?'

'Actually, I'd rather come to you. Don't want the neighbours asking questions,' she chuckled.

'Right. This is an urgent matter, are you able to come this evening?' Barrett was not going to take no for an answer.

'Let me just settle my kids and then I'll come. Is that OK?'

'Yes, but while I have you on the phone, would you mind giving me a list of all the people who attended the book club?'

'Oh, yeah. Sure. There was nine of us, I think …' Kim counted on her fingers. 'Yeah, nine including Toni.'

'Their names, please,' Barrett encouraged, gritting his teeth.

'Right, it was at Marion's house. Marion Bolton. I was there ...' Barrett held his breath. This wasn't going at the speed he would have liked. 'Then there was Barbara Lipton, Amy Martin, Maggie Barnsdale, Pauline Robinson, Shirley Grubb and Janet Cox.'

Barrett scribbled down the names and waved the piece of paper across the room at Palmer.

'That's very helpful, Mrs Geller.'

'I'll get the kids down and then I'll come over.'

'Thank you. Please ask for DCI Barrett at the front desk when you arrive.'

'Will do,' she said in a singsong voice before hanging up the phone.

'I want you to track down Marion Bolton first. She hosted the book club. We need to speak to her.' Barrett had slammed down the phone and was barking orders at Palmer. 'Mrs Geller is going to come to the station later. In the meantime, get on with this.' He thrust the piece of paper listing the book group members' names at Palmer.

After two cups of coffee, Kim got in a taxi and went to Parkside police station. As she stepped out of the silver Mercedes she felt her stomach knot. She'd never had to give a statement before and she felt nervous.

The officer at the front desk looked up as she breezed into the station, doing her best to disguise her nerves.

'I've come to speak to DCI Barrett.' She smiled her most innocent smile.

The ginger-haired officer blushed before picking up the phone and calling the incident room.

'He'll be down in a minute,' the officer told her, hanging up the phone. 'Take a seat over there.'

Kim nodded and did as she was told. A minute later DCI Barrett arrived.

'Mrs Geller?' he said, extending his hand.

'Yes.' They shook hands and he was surprised by how attractive she was. 'Good to meet you.'

'Thank you for agreeing to speak with me.'

'Anything I can do to help,' she said, wishing she wasn't so eager to please.

'Are any of the interview rooms free?' Barrett leant over and asked the officer at the desk.

'Yes, sir. Room three is available.'

From somewhere else in the station Kim heard a man shouting, and hoped they wouldn't be going anywhere near the holding cells.

'Come with me,' Barrett said, leading the way into a small room. 'Have a seat.'

Barrett sat opposite her as Palmer appeared at the doorway to join them.

'This is DI Palmer,' Barrett introduced his colleague. 'As I said, thank you for offering to help with our enquiries. We'd like to start with you telling us how you knew the victim.' As Barrett sat back and crossed his arms across his chest, Kim noticed sweat marks on his white shirt.

'We met about six years ago. She was working at the gym, DW Fitness First. It's the one at the Beehive centre. After having the twins my stomach wasn't quite what it used to be.' She gave a naughty chuckle. 'So, I thought I'd join the gym and try to get my figure back. Toni was working on reception and we got chatting. I liked her. I thought she was spunky. Not too many like that around.'

'Was this before or after she met her second husband?' Palmer asked.

'Before. She had only just broken up with Mike. That's why she had that job. She hated it, but because they never had kids he didn't have to give her any money.'

'Do you know why the marriage ended?' Barrett leant in and put his hands on the table.

'At first she was telling me it was because he was an alcoholic, but one night, when we'd been out for a few drinks, she opened up and told me she'd had an affair.'

The officers looked at each other.

'I don't know who, though. She never told me. Used to freeze up any time I mentioned it, so I just stopped mentioning it.' Kim shrugged.

The disappointment showed on Barrett's face.

'Can you tell me about the evening Toni was killed? We want to try and work out her movements.'

'Well, we all met at Marion's house at six. I've told you that there were nine of us that night. The book club is bigger than that but we can't always all make it.' She looked down at her deep red sparkly nail varnish.

'She was already at Marion's when I arrived,' Kim reminisced. 'Babs arrived, then Shirley and Janet. Pauline was next. Amy and Maggie arrived just as Toni was about to storm out. We didn't even get a chance to talk about the book before it all kicked off.'

Barrett raised an eyebrow. 'There was an argument?'

'Yeah. Kind of.'

'Who was the argument between?'

'Kind of all of us.' Kim looked sheepish.

'Go on,' Barrett demanded.

'I dunno. Toni was in a prickly mood. Kept making little comments and I told her to watch her mouth.' Kim moved in her chair, making the plastic beneath her squeak.

'I see.'

'She could be a bitch sometimes. I'd always been there for her and I didn't get why she was being so harsh. Marion tried to calm everyone down but then I kind of erupted. Janet got involved and she and Toni said some pretty hurtful things to one another. Then I left.'

'You say she was in a prickly mood, can you describe what you mean?'

'She was someone who always thought of themselves as proper, do you know what I mean? Like, she thought she was better than other people. Special. She had a big ego, and I guess on that day I wasn't really in the mood to put up with it.'

'Was there any reason for that?' Palmer asked.

'Not really. She had a go at me about smoking, and obviously didn't approve that I'd brought a bottle of wine to the book club, even though we always have a few glasses, some of us. I was tired and didn't need her judging me. I basically told her so. If I'd known that would be the last time I'd see her ...' Her words faded.

'What time did Toni leave the meeting?'

'Probably around half six, I guess. After me, so I've been told.'

Barrett sat back and looked at Kim. She didn't look like a killer, and he'd met a few in his time, but he got the feeling that she was holding something back.

'And where did you go when you left?'

'I went to see my friend, Dawn. She lives over in Girton. We went to the pub, The George Inn, and then I went back and crashed at her place.'

'We'll need the contact details of your friend so we can corroborate your statement. What time did you arrive at her house?'

'Must have been around half seven.' Kim felt more nervous the longer the interview went on. 'I had nothing to do with Toni's death. It was just a silly little argument. We used to have them all the time. It didn't mean anything.'

Barrett looked at Palmer and gave a knowing nod.

'Well—' Barrett got up. 'Thank you for coming in. As I said, we'll need your friend's details. I'll be in touch if we need anything else.'

'OK.' Kim stood up hastily, grateful that the conversation was coming to an end.

Back in the incident room, Barrett looked cross: his brow was furrowed and he sat in his chair staring at the board on the wall.

There was something off about the case but he couldn't put his finger on it.

'How are you coming along with the names of the people who attended the book club?' he asked Palmer, who was glued to a computer screen.

'I'm getting there, sir.' Palmer was tapping at the keyboard furiously.

'There is something not right about this whole damn thing.' Barrett got up and went over to the board, which was a mess of photos, maps and scribbled writing.

'Normally, I'd want us to focus our attentions on the husband, but he has a cast iron alibi. It seems unlikely that the murder was as a result of a spat at a book club meeting.' He paced backwards and forwards with his hands behind his back. Palmer hated it when he did that. He found it extremely annoying.

'Should we consider the possibility of a serial?' Palmer said, quietly enough so that Barrett was the only person in the room who heard.

'There is no evidence of that, yet. The geraniums in her hair are an oddity, but I think there is something personal about this case. Unless another body shows up, there is no reason to suspect that is the case.'

'Apart from the geranium,' Palmer insisted, 'and,' he cleared his throat, 'the fact that her clothes were missing.'

'Yes. No sign of a sexual assault yet she was discovered naked. Where are the clothes? Why strip the body?' Barrett stood looking at the photograph of the body and cocked his head to one side. 'Humiliation,' he said thoughtfully.

'Excuse me, sir?'

'Well, if there was no sexual motivation behind the killing, by removing her clothes the killer has humiliated her. Look at the position of the body: face down, legs spread apart, bum on show. The body has been carefully arranged like that.'

'And with the petals,' Palmer added.

'Yes,' Barrett snapped, 'the damn petals too.'

'Could it be ritualistic?' Palmer got up and stood next to Barrett, looking at all the images from the crime scene.

'It would appear that despite the violence, this was not a sporadic attack. The killer would have had to have the flowers with them – in order to arrange the body like that. This was carefully planned.'

The incident room was hot and they were all tired. The hours they had to put in were always unforgiving when they were investigating a murder.

Barrett looked at his watch. It was 8.50pm. 'Let's order pizza,' he said, 'it's going to be a long night.'

Chapter 10

9.40pm 23 June

After enjoying a few slices of a Domino's pizza, Barrett and Palmer were back in the car on their way to visit Marion Bolton, in Cherry Hinton.

Darkness was beginning to fall and the moon hung in the sky like a fingernail clipping. Neither of the men spoke as they travelled through the city observing the Saturday night revellers on the streets of Cambridge. The station would be busy with drunks, and people who'd been in fights around closing time. It always was at the weekend.

They pulled up outside 33 Gladstone Way and got out of the car. The night air was warm, and as they approached the front door they were greeted by the scent of roses coming from the shrubs on the pristine front lawn.

Palmer was pleased to see there were lights on downstairs. He took no pleasure in disturbing sleeping pensioners.

'Hello?' A tall, slender, grey haired man opened the door.

'Good evening.' Barrett showed his badge. 'I'm looking for Marion Bolton. Is she here?'

'Yes.' The gentleman took the badge and inspected it. 'She is.'

'Can we come in please, sir?'

'What's wrong? What's happened?' He looked panicked.

'We need to ask Mrs Bolton some questions regarding the book club she is a member of.'

Alfred Bolton could not hide his confusion.

'You'd better come in,' he said, turning and calling out to his wife.

In the living room, they found Marion sitting on the sofa reading a book, and rugby on the television. Barrett enjoyed watching rugby and took a particular interest in the score before turning his attention to Marion.

'Good evening. I am sorry for disturbing you at this hour,' Palmer introduced himself. 'We are investigating the murder of Toni Jones. I understand you knew the victim?'

Marion put down her book and reached for the remote control and turned off the television off, much to Barrett's disappointment. Alfred took a seat next to his wife to show his support.

'Yes. That's right, I knew Toni. Awful thing that happened.' She shook her head and Alfred put a hand on her knee.

'We understand that on June twenty-first you hosted a book club meeting here, is that correct?'

'Yes. It was my turn.'

'Can you tell us what happened?'

'Well, these bloody girls, women, sorry, they bicker. It goes on and on and that day was no different. I don't think they really like each other a lot of them, but we have to try and rub along because of the club. I told them to pack it in but Kim ended up leaving, followed by Toni. She wasn't too happy.' Marion proceeded to repeat almost exactly the same story as Kim had, while Palmer took notes. 'There was a lot of tension that day. More than usual, I suppose,' she continued.

'Why do you think that was?' Palmer pressed.

'Well.' Marion looked at her feet for a moment, seemingly considering her slippers. 'It's complicated.'

Barrett held his breath. Maybe this would be the moment all the pieces fell into place.

'I'd found something out. Something awful.' She looked at Alfred who gave an encouraging nod. 'Toni had recently had an abortion.'

Neither Palmer nor Barrett's face gave anything away. The pathologist had also discovered this and had shared the discovery with them earlier that day.

'How did you find this out?'

'My son, Harry, his girlfriend Erica works at the clinic. She told me, because she was worried about Toni. They'd met at my seventieth birthday party and got chatting. Erica recognised her the minute she saw her at the clinic.'

The policemen waited patiently for her to continue.

'I don't want Erica getting in trouble. She is a kind girl. She said that Toni came in on her own and left on her own.' Marion paused. 'Gerald wasn't with her. This was about four weeks ago.'

'Did you mention this to Mrs Jones?'

'Well, actually no. Not to begin with.' Marion appeared embarrassed. 'I didn't know what to say, and, like I said, I didn't want to get Erica in trouble. But I was worried. Toni was a proud person, but I felt she'd seemed out of sorts for a while so I arranged to have a coffee with her. She thought I wanted to talk about the book club. She was horrified when I said I knew about the termination.' She spoke with a troubled expression on her face. 'She swore me to secrecy, made me promise I wouldn't breathe a word. I told her that her secret was safe with me, but asked her why she'd done it.' Marion sucked in a long breath. 'She started to cry. I'd never seen her vulnerable, I didn't know what to do. Then she told me the baby wasn't Gerald's.'

'Did she tell you who the father was?'

'No. She refused.' Marion paused. 'But there's more. She told me she had been raped.' The statement hung in the air like a poisonous gas. 'I got the impression she knew the man – just the way she seemed to want to protect his identity. It was odd.'

'This was never reported to the police,' Barrett added.

'No. I know. She said she just wanted to forget about it. We only spoke about it the once. I never said anything more to her.'

'Were you aware that Toni had an affair while she was married to Mike Williams?' Marion's cheeks flushed slightly red.

'Not me.' She got up from the sofa. 'Can I offer you tea, or something else to drink?'

'No, thank you, Mrs Bolton. We're almost done with our questions.' Barrett encouraged her to return to the couch, but the woman remained where she was.

'I've told you all that I know.' Palmer could see her shutters were coming down. 'She was a complicated woman, not everyone's cup of tea, but I don't know why she was killed.'

Realising they weren't going to get any more out of her, Barrett also stood.

'Here is my card,' he said, handing it over. 'You've been very helpful.'

'You will be delicate with what I told you?' Marion's eyes were full of concern.

'Absolutely,' Palmer interjected.

'If you think of anything else that might be relevant, please give us a call. Thank you both for your time this evening, we won't keep you any longer.'

'You were right to keep a lid on the abortion, sir.'

'I had a feeling it would surface sooner or later.' Barrett looked smug as he pulled his seatbelt on.

'We've still no idea who the father was, though,' Palmer commented.

'Wrong, Joe, we know more than we did. We know for certain it wasn't her husband, and we know the victim claimed she was raped.'

'True, but that doesn't exactly narrow it down.'

'I thought Mrs Bolton's comment about it being someone Toni knew was interesting. She's a wily old bird. I bet she doesn't miss a trick.'

'Yes. Did you notice how she clammed up when you asked her about the affair?' Palmer said, starting the car.

'I did, Joe, I did indeed.' Barrett strummed his fingers on his knee. 'Right, back to the station. Let's hope there is still some pizza left.'

'You did the right thing, love.' Alfred handed over a cup of hot cocoa to his wife as she stood in the kitchen looking out at the moonlit garden.

'I don't know. What if Erica ends up in trouble? I'd never want that.'

'I know. I got the feeling that they were going to be very discreet. It's not in their interest to land Erica in trouble with work. They just want to find out everything they can about Toni.'

'It's Gerald I feel sorry for.' Marion sipped her drink.

'Yes, poor chap.'

'She wasn't a good wife to Mike and she was never very nice to Gerald, but he did love her. He must be devastated. Perhaps tomorrow I'll pay him a visit.'

'Do you think that's wise?' Alfred's words were loaded with caution.

'Why ever not?' Marion blinked.

'Well, you knew stuff about his wife.' He let the statement hang in the air. 'I just don't want you getting caught up in this. You have to take care of yourself. Especially with your blood pressure.'

'You daft bugger.' Marion put down her cup and wrapped her arms around her husband. 'You don't need to worry about me.'

'But I do, love.' He planted a kiss on the top of her head and they remained embracing for a moment. 'I think you did the right thing not saying anything about the affair.'

Marion looked up at her husband. 'It's not my job to destroy someone else's marriage.'

'No, it's not,' Alfred paused, 'but there may come a time when you do have to say something.'

'I really hope not,' she sighed. 'Enough people have been hurt already without me sticking my beak in.'

'I have faith you'll do the right thing.' He smiled down at his wife. 'You're a good woman, Marion Bolton.'

'And you're a good man, Alfred Bolton.' She squeezed his waist. 'I'm lucky to have you.'

Back in the incident room Palmer and Barrett were disappointed to discover the pizza had been finished.

'OK,' Barrett clapped his hands, 'listen up. We've spoken to Marion Bolton, who hosted the book club on the night Toni Jones died. She told us that Toni Jones was raped, and that was the reason for the abortion. At this stage, I have no reason to believe that Mrs Bolton is lying. Tomorrow, I want to speak to Erica …' he checked his notes, 'Clutterbuck.' A snigger went around the room. 'Yes, yes,' Barrett dismissed the giggles. 'Erica works at the clinic on Bateman Street. She witnessed Mrs Jones arriving for her termination. Now, I don't need to remind you that this is a very delicate situation. This information needs to be handled with the strictest confidence. I need to talk to Erica in the morning. For now, I want you to look into Mrs Jones' medical records. See if you can find anything that might be of interest.' Heads nodded around the room. 'Back to work.'

Barrett returned to his office, summoning Elly Hale and Palmer as he went.

'You two,' he said, sitting down at his desk and folding his hands together, 'I want you both to go and interview Erica tomorrow. I want to know if Toni said anything about who might have fathered the child. I want to know how far into the pregnancy she was. Visit Erica Clutterbuck at her home. I don't want this getting out yet.'

'Yes, sir.' This was Elly Hale's first murder investigation and she was keen to be as involved as possible. 'Sir, if you don't mind me saying, I think it would be wise for me to lead the interview.' Her boldness surprised Barrett and Palmer.

'Good point.' Barrett rubbed his chin. 'Do your best.' He dismissed her with a wave of his hand.

'I will pay a visit to Janet Cox. We know she had an altercation with the victim the evening of her death. I need to build up a picture of Toni's movements that night. They are being cagey, some of these women, and I want to get to the bottom of it.'

'Yes, sir.'

'How's the examination of her computer coming along?' Barrett tapped his pen on the table.

'We are getting there. There are a lot of messages to read through. If anything significant is discovered, you'll be the first to know.'

Palmer paused in the doorway. 'Sir, tomorrow is my son's eighth birthday. It would mean a lot to him if I could be at his party, just for a little while.'

'When is it?'

'It starts at four.' Palmer looked sheepish as Barrett sighed and rubbed his temples. 'He's meeting his friends on Jesus Green and they are going to have a kick around and then a picnic. I don't need to stay for the whole thing.'

'I can spare you for half an hour, but I need every man, and woman,' Barrett corrected himself, 'to have their full attention on this case.'

'Half an hour would be great, thank you, sir. I'll make the hours up.'

'We've got our backs to the wall with this one. It's going to be very difficult to prove that Toni was raped, if she was, and since no one wants to spill the beans on who she was having an affair with, for now, we aren't any closer to discovering the motive.' Palmer could see that Barrett had one of his headaches coming on.

'We made progress tonight, sir.'

'Not enough,' Barrett growled.

Chapter 11

7am 24th June

Having left the station at 1am, Elly Hale appeared looking bright-eyed and bushy-tailed at 7am on Sunday morning. Barrett was wearing the same clothes and had clearly only slept for a few hours on the sofa in his office. Palmer was running late.

'Sir,' Elly said as she handed her boss a cup of hot coffee, 'it occurred to me last night that the date of the murder might be significant.'

'Why's that?' Barrett blew on his drink.

'Well, it is the date of the summer solstice. June twenty-first was the longest day this calendar year.'

'And?' Barrett was not in a very forgiving mood.

'Well, it might just be something to consider,' she suggested, but Barrett didn't respond and she left the office feeling dejected. She sat at her desk waiting impatiently for Palmer to arrive. She'd been keen to get to work that morning, but since her little chat with Barrett she wished she was at home, snuggled up in bed with her boyfriend.

Palmer arrived at seven-thirty and he too appeared to be in a foul mood.

'Good morning.' Elly tried to sound bright.

'Is it?' He huffed, plonking himself in his chair and switching on his computer. *Great*, Elly thought to herself, *that's two grumpy buggers and it's not yet eight o'clock.*

'I've got an address for Erica Clutterbuck.' She smiled, intent on not allowing him to bring her down. 'She lives in Great Chesterford.'

'We'll head there at eight.' Palmer's eyes never left his screen.

'Very well, sir,' she said, gritting her teeth, wondering what had plunged Palmer into such a bad mood, and returning to her desk to nurse the watery black coffee she'd got herself from the machine in the hallway.

Twenty minutes later, Elly and Palmer were on Carmel Street in Great Chesterford – a bustling village on the Essex and Cambridgeshire border, twelve miles south of the city.

The sky above them was grey, and Palmer muttered something about hoping it wasn't going to rain as they approached a semi-detached white cottage. A dog barked from inside when they rang the doorbell, and a few moments later a sleepy-eyed woman appeared in her dressing gown. She did not look very happy to have been woken up.

'Miss Erica Clutterbuck?' Elly flashed her badge. 'I'm DS Hale. Sorry for disturbing you so early, but we have a few questions. I wonder if we could come in?' At Erica's heels a Jack Russell continued to yap.

Wiping the sleep from her eyes, and tightening the cord on her dressing gown so she didn't end up flashing the police, Erica nodded and yawned before sliding back the door into the cottage with her foot.

In the kitchen, there were a number of empty wine bottles and a few used glasses on the table, which were clearly from the previous night.

'It was my birthday.' Erica waved a hand in the direction of the empties, but made no attempt to tidy them up.

'Like I said, we're sorry to disturb you so early, but we are investigating the recent murder of a woman in Cambridge.'

'Oh.' The pieces suddenly fell into place for Erica. 'Toni Jones. That's what you're here about?'

'Yes.'

'I could lose my job.' Erica was now wide awake.

'We have no interest in talking to your employers, we simply want to know about the ...' she paused, 'appointment Mrs Jones had at the clinic you work at.'

Looking relieved, Erica pulled up a seat, being sure to secure her dressing gown once more. Her shoulder length, dark blonde hair could do with a brush, Palmer thought.

'I'm a nurse,' she explained. 'I've worked at the clinic for a while.'

Elly sat down opposite Erica and nodded encouragingly.

'About four or five weeks ago, maybe even six, I saw Mrs Jones at the clinic. She was extremely embarrassed when she recognised me. I approached her and said that I was not allowed to discuss my work outside of the clinic walls.' Erica's face flushed with guilt. 'I'd met her at Marion Bolton's birthday party – Marion is my boyfriend's mother.' Erica picked up the Jack Russell and placed the small dog on her knee.

Both officers remained quiet; neither of them were going to let on that it was Marion who had given them Erica's name.

'Anyway, like a lot of women who come into the clinic, she was pretty distressed, but she seemed more concerned by the fact that I'd seen her than what she was there for.'

'Did she discuss the pregnancy with you at all?' Elly asked gently, trying to ignore the pungent scent of red wine and Chinese takeaway that hung in the air.

'I'm really not sure I can say.'

'Miss Clutterbuck, this is a murder investigation. It is vital that we get a picture of the mental state of the victim during the weeks leading up to her death.' Palmer was not prepared to be so gentle.

'And I've not even had a cup of tea yet.' Erica rolled her eyes.

'Did she mention who the father was?' Palmer asked.

'She said she had been raped. It was strange, because I didn't ask. We are told not to pry. She just came out and said it.'

'Did she say who by?'

'No. I didn't push her. That's not my job. I, of course, encouraged her to go to the police but she said she wouldn't. She said she knew her attacker and that she wanted to leave the past in the past. I didn't really understand what she meant.'

'Can you tell us how far along with the pregnancy Mrs Jones was?'

'Yes. She was approximately eight weeks.'

'Is there anything else you think may be relevant?' Palmer put his hands in his pockets and fumbled with the car keys.

'Not really. She didn't seem concerned by the procedure though, just more concerned that someone she knew was aware she was having it.'

'Thank you very much, Miss Clutterbuck, you've been very helpful. If we have any further questions, we'll be in touch.' Elly got up from the kitchen chair.

'No problem.' Erica stifled a yawn behind her hand and scooped the dog up under her arm. It proceeded to try and lick her chin.

'We'll see ourselves out.' Elly reached out a hand and ruffled the fur under the dog's neck.

As soon as she heard the front door close, Erica went back upstairs to bed, closely followed by her canine companion.

Shirley hated having to work weekends, but as a carer at a nursing home she didn't have much choice. The shifts were on a rota, and that Sunday it was her turn to do a weekend day shift.

Leaving Kayla and Grant both sleeping in their beds, she got into her small blue Fiat, in a bad mood, and drove from her house on Rawlyn Road to the Hinton Grange Care Home in Cherry Hinton.

On her journey she listened to the radio in an attempt to cheer herself up, but even the happy beat from the pop songs that played couldn't lift her mood, and the low grey clouds outside did nothing to help.

As she pulled her car into the care home car park she angrily turned off the radio, more irritated by the music than soothed by it, and pulled the car into a parking space.

Shirley sat for a moment, looking at the building she worked in. It looked particularly depressing when the sky was grey and, despite the pretence that it was a happy place, the weather reflected the reality.

Getting out of the car, she straightened her uniform and made her way into the home.

An elderly man who was suffering with severe Alzheimer's was in the corridor, trying to walk with the aid of a Zimmer frame. By his side was Maxine, another nurse at the home, making sure he didn't topple over. Maxine looked at Shirley and welcomed her with a warm smile that was not reciprocated.

Despite the best efforts of the cleaning staff, the place still had a strange smell of age and death. Shirley hated it but she needed the job. Grant's salary alone was not enough for them to live on. Marrying a window cleaner had not been in Shirley's plans, but life had a funny way of throwing up surprises.

Shirley entered the staffroom and went over to the board to check who she would be in charge of that day. To her disappointment she saw she was on bedpan duties, and her list included a number of male residents. As Shirley wrapped the blue polythene apron around her large waist, she cursed her recent luck.

For a while, life had been good enough, but recently she had felt stressed and unhappy. She disliked her job and when she was at home she had to contend with a spoilt, difficult daughter, who constantly reminded her that she wasn't her biological mother. Shirley was a lot of things but she wasn't thick. She found herself looking at her life and wondering where it had all gone wrong.

Grant was a useless husband. He didn't provide enough money, spent a lot of time at the pub with his friends, spoiled their daughter – making her life harder, and never did any of the things he promised he would, like fixing the leaking tap or repapering the dining room with the wallpaper she'd bought three months earlier.

On the odd occasion, she found herself feeling jealous of the old folk she looked after. No one ever looked after her. She was a skivvy at home, just as she was at work.

She loved Kayla, but the girl was difficult. Shirley had always made the excuse that it was because Kayla had a hang-up, as a result of being adopted, but in recent days she had found herself wondering if it was simply that Kayla wasn't a very nice person. They had known very little about her biological parents. Perhaps they weren't good people, and perhaps the apple didn't fall so far from the tree.

Shirley met Grant when she was eighteen and by the time she was nineteen they were married. She had left school at sixteen and was working in a factory, packing meat, when they met. He was six years older and was her supervisor.

Desperate to move away from home, Shirley had jumped at Grant's marriage proposal, and decided at the same time that she'd take a nursing course. Encouraged by her desire to better herself, Grant also quit working at the factory, and set up his own window cleaning business. They couple were broke but happy, and quickly wanted to have a baby. But after three years of trying, they paid a visit to their doctor, and after a few examinations it was concluded that Shirley was infertile due to a uterine abnormality.

The distraught couple soon decided they would adopt, and they put themselves forward. It took two years before they were awarded their little bundle, whom they named Kayla.

Grant doted on his little girl and she had him wrapped around her little finger. During their first few years together the family were happy, but as Kayla grew she became strong-willed and had soon built a wedge between the husband and wife. To Grant, Kayla could do no wrong, but Shirley wanted the girl to grow up learning manners and respect. 'Don't be so hard on her', Grant would say if Shirley ever attempted to hold her child to account for her behaviour. Soon enough, rather than fight Grant, Shirley stopped trying as Kayla grew more and more unpleasant.

Now, at thirty-eight years old, Shirley spent her time at home trying to placate her teenage daughter, and her time at work trying to placate the elderly residents she was paid a poor salary to care for.

As Shirley filled the bedpan with warm, soapy water she wished she was someone else. She'd not been on holiday for as long as she could remember, and hoped it was possible that she and Grant could save enough to go to Blackpool with Kayla for a few nights in the summer. She used to visit the seaside resort as a child and had fond memories of the place.

Pushing the bedpan trolley along the corridor, Shirley made her way to the first resident on her list: Frank Moult. Pushing open the heavy fire-retardant door, she huffed as she entered. Frank lay on his bed, frail and motionless. She stopped for a moment and fixed her eyes on his chest. There was movement and she breathed a sigh of relief. Finding dead residents was part of the job.

'Morning, Frank.' She spoke loudly, waking him from his slumber with no gentleness. The old man opened his sunken blue eyes, and his mind tried to bring him into the present.

'Time for your bath.' She snapped on the latex gloves, not looking forward to the task ahead.

The old man didn't make any attempt to move and looked like a small bird, sinking into the pillows under his head. Frank was confined to his bed. His legs had given up working properly some months before.

'Up you sit.' Shirley hooked her arm under his and hoisted him up the bed. The old man appeared surprised by the sudden, rough movement.

'Come on. Take it off.' She pointed a gloved finger at his crumpled, striped nightshirt. 'I've got others to see to.'

With quivering hands he tried to undo the buttons, but his swollen arthritic fingers were not capable of the job.

Sighing impatiently, Shirley batted his hand out of the way and worked her way down the line of buttons before pulling the shirt off him. His body was sunken and she could see his ribs and sternum beneath a few wiry, white chest hairs.

Plunging the sponge into the now tepid water, she washed his back and upper body before roughly patting him dry with a towel. Next, she pulled back the bedding and removed his stained white underpants, making no attempt to hide the revulsion on her face. Embarrassed by the marks on his underwear, the old man hung his head in shame while she wiped around his genitals. This was Shirley's least favourite part of the job and it was only the first one of the day. She had six more to get through before the morning was done.

Instead of looking for a fresh pair, Shirley put Frank's soiled underwear back on him. She pulled on his nightshirt, only doing up every other button, and covered him with the bedsheet before leaving his room. She didn't say goodbye or offer him a smile as she left, and the door slammed loudly behind her leaving Frank alone once again, a prisoner in his room.

By the time she had finished bathing all the residents on her list, Shirley was red-faced and angry. Not wanting to spend time talking to the other staff, she took her egg sandwich and bag of salt and vinegar crisps and sat alone on the wall outside the front of the nursing home. Above, the clouds had darkened and the wind was beginning to pick up, blowing rubbish from one of the bins playfully across the car park.

Despite the unforgiving weather, Shirley ate her lunch as slowly as she could, being sure to make the most of her break. The egg sandwich had been made the night before and as a result the bread was slightly soggy, but she was hungry after her morning's work and she ate it all regardless.

Not in the mood for small talk with her colleagues, she decided she'd take herself for a walk around the grounds to ensure she used the full hour of her lunch. She didn't care if it was about to rain: nothing could make her feel lower than she did already.

*

Across the city, Janet was preparing to go to work. Paddy Power, the bookies, opened its doors at 9am – even on Sunday. One small blessing was that she lived in the small two-bedroomed flat above the shop and didn't have far to travel to work.

After she'd opened up, she sat in her chair to read a book, waiting for the first punter to arrive. The job gave her plenty of opportunity to read, which was why she never grumbled about it. That, twinned with the fact she had left school at sixteen, was pregnant by seventeen, and had no qualifications, meant she had to take work wherever she could get it.

She'd been working at Paddy Power for the last seven years and now owned the proud title of manager. In reality, all that meant was that she was responsible for cashing up and locking up, but Janet was content with the simple things in life. She was not ambitious.

That Sunday was just like every other, and by 9.30am her first customer had appeared. There were a number of regulars who she'd got to know, which also made the job more bearable, even if most of them were losers or drunks. Janet had seen enough tragic men to fill her lifetime and had sworn herself to celibacy some years before.

Her nineteen-year-old son, Dean, spent as little time at home with his mother as he could. He'd never met his father and resented his single mother. He spent most of his time hanging out with friends, getting into trouble, when he wasn't working at KFC. It was obvious to those who knew them that Dean had as many aspirations as his mother.

The young man had already been in trouble with the police, on numerous occasions: twice for carrying drugs, once for joyriding – for which he received a suspended sentence – and once for ABH, after getting into a fight outside a pub.

Janet loved her son but had neither the will nor the desire to deal with him. He was disrespectful and occasionally she had wished that his father was on the scene. In truth though, Janet had not seen Dean's father since she was a teenager. She'd got drunk at a party and one thing had led to another. Five months later she'd discovered she was pregnant, but it was too late to do anything about it. Her Catholic mother and father kicked her out for bringing shame on them and Janet had been alone in life ever since. It was one of the reasons she had such a love for reading. It filled her days and helped stop the feeling of loneliness – that was what had led her to start her online book blog. She ploughed many hours into reading and reviewing and soon began to gather a small following. It was as a result of her blog that she'd met Shirley, three years ago. When the women realised they were local to one another they arranged to meet for coffee, and had been good friends ever since.

As was always the case, by 11am the shop was beginning to get busy and Janet's attention was drawn away from her Kindle.

She served the regulars and watched them leave empty-handed – with miserable faces as usual. When Pauline walked in, wearing dark glasses, Janet couldn't hide her surprise. Pauline, when she noticed Janet standing behind the counter, looked equally shocked, and she contemplated turning around and walking out, pretending she hadn't seen her book club companion. But, realising it was too late, she decided to brave it out.

'What are you doing here?' Janet whistled.

'Oh, erm … I just …' Pauline removed her glasses to reveal her eyes, which darted around, unwilling to meet Janet's. 'It's for Roger.' Roger was Pauline's husband.

'Oh. Didn't know he was a gambler.' Janet was not about to let Pauline off the hook so lightly. 'What you betting on?'

Pauline looked over at the televisions on the wall and the digital table of odds, and her puffy eyes filled with tears.

'You alright?' Janet leant so far forward towards the glass that her breath appeared on it in a fog.

'Not really.' Pauline's whole body was shaking, which made the sunglasses on top of her head look unstable.

'I'm not meant to do this, but, come round.' Janet signalled to the door that gave access to employees who worked the tills. Pauline nodded gratefully and she slipped around the side. Janet lifted the latch, which kept her and the money she took daily, safe, and let Pauline in. She was dabbing her eyes with a tissue that she'd removed from her brown leather handbag.

'I didn't mean to upset you,' Janet sniffed, feeling a pang of guilt.

'It's not your fault. Everything is just such a mess.' She collapsed on a tatty beige office chair, which groaned under the weight of her wide hips. Janet chewed her crusty bottom lip, while keeping half an eye on the punters standing around in the shop.

'I don't know where it all went wrong.' Pauline sniffed back more tears. 'It started off as a good idea.' Janet nodded, not having a clue what Pauline was talking about. 'The business, it's sinking.'

Janet had a vague recollection of Pauline talking about a business that she and Roger had started, but couldn't for the life of her remember anything about it. 'It was such a good idea. It could have set us up for our retirement. That was the plan.' Pauline looked at the rose gold wedding ring on her finger and started to fiddle with it.

'Get it off your chest.' Janet managed to sound sincere, even if she was only asking out of nosiness.

'Well, you know, the van cost us a lot of money, but we saw it as an investment.' Suddenly, it all came flooding back to Janet. Pauline and her husband, Roger, had bought a van and wanted to set up a mobile library. Now, this in itself wasn't a new idea, but Pauline had had the brainwave of lending Kindles rather than paperbacks. The idea was that borrowers would request the book they wanted and, rather than storing hundreds of physical books, it would be downloaded to an eBook device.

Roger, who had been a teacher, was retired, and when Pauline stopped working at WH Smith she'd had the brainwave to start the business. It had been something she'd been considering for a while.

Determined to make a real go of it, the couple had mortgaged their house and bought an expensive state-of-the-art van and a vast number of Kindles. Roger had no real passion for books but was enthusiastic about the business potential. After splashing the cash, the business had hit a bump in the road. The minor detail that Pauline had overlooked, was that people were perfectly capable of buying their own Kindles and downloading the books themselves. Within a year of starting the business they had found themselves in serious financial difficulty.

Pauline explained to Janet that they were struggling to keep up with the mortgage repayments, and their house was close to being repossessed. Janet sat, stunned, listening to the mess the aging couple had got themselves into.

'But why are you here?' Janet scratched her dry scalp.

'It's my last throw of the dice,' Pauline added miserably. 'My daughter has given us two thousand pounds to help us keep up with the payments, but she can't afford to keep bailing us out. I thought, maybe, just maybe, I might be able to double our pot.' Pauline hung her head in shame for a second time that morning, while Janet sat and chewed on the sleeve of her faded blue top.

After a long silence, Pauline quietly said, 'You won't tell anyone about this, will you?'

Janet looked, sadly, at someone she had once respected as a proud, astute woman.

'No. I won't tell anyone.'

'Thank you.' Pauline cleared her throat and sat more upright.

'What you going to do then?' Pauline watched out of the corner of her eye, as one of the regular punters crumbled when his horse didn't finish the race.

'I'm going to roll the dice one last time.' Pauline removed a fat wad of cash from her bag. 'Any tips?' Her eyes were pleading.

'I don't gamble.' Janet shook her head slowly. 'But,' she added thoughtfully, 'if I was going to, I'd not do it on horses. I think football is a safer bet.'

'I don't know anything about football,' Pauline said, turning up her nose.

'I don't suppose you do,' Janet mused, 'but lucky for you, a few of the fellas who come into the shop, do.' She nodded in the direction of a tall man who was standing hunched over a betting slip, with a rolled-up cigarette tucked behind his ear.

'He's a winner,' Janet winked. Pauline, looking the man up and down, would certainly not have described him as that.

'World Cup's on at the moment. Have a word with Jim. He knows a thing or two.' Janet returned to the till to take the money off yet another helpless soul who was hoping to win big.

'Thank you for listening.' Pauline got up and pulled her sunglasses back down over her eyes.

'No worries. Our little secret.' Janet grinned, showing yellow teeth. 'Just a word of advice though, no matter how bad it gets, just be grateful you've got your health. Poor old Toni ain't.'

'Yes, well.' Pauline stiffened.

'What is it?' Janet's eyes narrowed.

'That woman is partly responsible for my situation. I can't say I'm sad she's dead.'

'Responsible how?' Janet paused, holding the change she was meant to hand over to the man on the other side of the till.

'She encouraged me. Said it was a great idea. Said she and Gerald would invest money and swore blind it would happen. She helped pick the van, came up with the marketing – she told me her sister was in marketing, and would come up with a plan for us, but when it came to putting money in, suddenly she went quiet. We'd already signed the agreement with the garage. They were meant to split the monthly repayments with us, fifty-fifty. I trusted her.' Pauline's voice wavered. 'She said we would be in it together, but when it came to the crunch she was only interested in looking after herself.'

'Well.' Janet took her time to process the new information. 'You kept that quiet.'

'What could I say?' A tear ran down from beneath the sunglasses. 'Look, I'd rather this stayed between us. I don't want anyone else to know.' *I bet you don't*, thought Janet, putting the pieces of the puzzle together.

'Did you have an agreement or anything? Anything on paper?'

'No,' Pauline said so quietly, Janet had to strain to hear her. 'And now Roger and I are on the brink of losing everything.'

Chapter 12

11am 24 June

Elly and Palmer returned to Parkside police station just as the rain broke.

'It probably won't last,' Elly said enthusiastically, after Palmer told her about his son's planned birthday party that afternoon.

Palmer, who had a face like thunder, was not going to allow himself to be hopeful.

The incident room was a flurry of activity as he made his way towards Barrett's office.

Barrett was hunched over his desk, carefully inspecting sheets of notes.

'Come in.' He waved his hand without looking up.

'We spoke to Ms Clutterbuck, sir. She confirms that the victim also told her she was raped.'

'Name?'

'No name, sir. Ms Clutterbuck did say that she got the feeling the victim was more concerned that she'd been recognised than she was about the procedure.'

'Right. Come here. Some new information has come to light.' Barrett thrust some papers towards Palmer, which had lines highlighted in fluorescent pen. Palmer accepted the paperwork and sat on a chair against the wall, scanning the highlighted messages.

'We lifted this from Mrs Jones' computer. The messages you see are between her and someone called Pauline Robinson. She was a member of the book club, who I have confirmed was there the night the victim was murdered.'

Palmer continued reading.

PAULINE ROBINSON: Where is the money?

TONI JONES: I haven't got it.

PAULINE ROBINSON: Why not?

TONI JONES: Gerald won't give me any.

PAULINE ROBINSON: You promised. You said you were on board. I can't do this without your help. You've screwed us.

TONI JONES: Don't be so over dramatic.

PAULINE ROBINSON: I beg your pardon? How dare you.

TONI JONES: You can't lay the blame on me. I tried, but Gerald doesn't think the business is viable. I happen to agree.

PAULINE JONES: You could have told me that before I agreed to purchase a van and committed myself to huge monthly repayments, which YOU said you'd share.

TONI JONES: Things change. I'm entitled to change my mind.

PAULINE ROBINSON: You can't play with people's lives like that.

TONI JONES: I can do exactly as I please. It's your fault you went ahead   and signed the papers without double-checking first.

PAULINE ROBINSON: You're unbelievable.

TONI JONES: I'll take that as a compliment.

PAULINE ROBINSON: Do you have any idea what you've done?

TONI JONES: I'm sorry you think you've been treated badly but you can't lay the blame on me.

PAULINE ROBINSON: I most certainly can. Where on earth do you think I am going to find the money to repay the loan?

TONI JONES: Not my problem.

PAULINE ROBINSON: I owe 34k thanks to you. We were meant to share that. You owe me 17k and I want my money. And that's before we've even spent the money on gutting the campervan to make it suitable!

TONI JONES: No chance.

PAULINE ROBINSON: You will pay. One way or another.
TONI JONES: Don't threaten me.
PAULINE ROBINSON: It's not a threat. It's a promise.

'Phew.' Palmer put down the notes. 'Strong stuff.'

'It's certainly a motive.' Barrett rubbed his chin. 'We need to speak to Pauline Robinson and her husband. Get your coat, Joe,' Barrett said, not noticing that Palmer hadn't yet had a chance to take it off since returning from his last excursion.

'We have the address.' Palmer got up and followed his boss out of the office.

'You're driving,' Barrett said, grimacing as he looked out of the window at the downpour.

Pauline and Roger Robinson lived at 37 Otter Close, in a cul-de-sac in the small town of Bar Hill, just northwest of the city. As they pulled up on the concrete strip in front of the house, the detectives' eyes were drawn to a surprising number of gnomes that were lined up on the windowsills and by the front door.

'Tacky bits of crap, if you ask me,' Palmer said, getting out of the car.

'Not my taste either, Joe.' Barrett looked up at the dark sky, grateful that the rain had abated for a while.

Before they had chance to get to the door it opened, and a short, fat man peered out at them.

'This is private property.' He frowned at them.

'Mr Robinson? DCI Barrett. We'd like to have a word with you and your wife.'

Roger, who clearly felt small in their presence, straightened his back and puffed out his chest.

'May I ask why?'

'I think it would be best if we discuss this indoors,' Barrett said, approaching. 'Is your wife at home?'

'She is.' He tucked his hands into the pockets of his grey trousers. 'She's just got back from church.'

Something to repent, perhaps? Palmer wondered.

'Please take your shoes off,' Roger instructed – himself wearing a comfortable pair of slippers.

Barrett always found it unnerving, having to interview strangers while wearing his socks with no shoes. He didn't like it one bit, but he grudgingly agreed and began to untie the laces on his black leather shoes. Palmer slipped out of his brogues, revealing odd socks. Barrett wouldn't be caught dead in odd socks and he looked at Palmer's feet with disapproval.

'Pauline,' Roger bellowed, 'the police are here and want to talk to us.'

Pauline appeared in the kitchen doorway holding a tea towel and a mug covered in suds. She too was wearing a pair of less than fetching slippers. His and hers, Barrett noted.

'Oh.' The colour drained from her podgy face. 'I'll come through in a moment.'

'Gentlemen.' Roger led them through into the living room, which was adorned with delicate china figures of Victorian women in elaborate robes. Barrett could never imagine living with such things and thanked his lucky stars he was a single man.

Pauline came into the room and stood awkwardly next to her husband. 'This is about Toni Jones, I presume.' Her husband looked tiny next to the tall woman.

'Yes, it is. I'd like to know when you last saw Mrs Jones.' Barrett, refusing to sit on the sofa, stood, eyeballing Pauline.

'Well, as I'm sure you probably know, I saw her at book club at Marion Bolton's house, the day she died.'

'Yes, and what time did you leave Mrs Bolton's home?'

'Oh.' Pauline looked at Roger. 'I think I was home in time for tea at about seven. That's right, isn't it?'

'Yes, I'd say so,' Roger said evenly. 'We got takeaway fish and chips.'

'Where did you get the fish and chips from?'

'I went to Churchill's fish and chips. We have fish every Friday,' Roger added, pushing home the idea that they were a traditional couple. 'I like cod, but Pauline always has haddock.'

'What time did you collect the order?' Palmer asked.

'Maybe, half past seven.'

'And you went to pick up the takeaway together?'

'No, I went alone,' Roger admitted.

'So where were you, Mrs Robinson?' Barrett tried to push away the lyrics of the song that entered his mind.

'I was on my way back.'

'A moment ago, you said you were at home.'

'Well, I was home in time for tea, yes.' She began to stumble over her words.

'What time did you return with the food?' Barrett turned his attention to Roger.

'Probably eight o'clock. By the time I'd placed the order and returned home, I'd say it was around then.'

'And your wife was at home when you returned?'

'Yes,' the couple said, in unison.

'So, you arrived home approximately between seven-twenty and eight o'clock, is that correct?' Palmer jotted down on his notepad.

'That sounds right,' Pauline agreed.

'But a moment ago you said you were at home by seven o'clock,' Barrett cut in.

'Approximately. I couldn't remember exactly.' Pauline looked like a woman caught with her pants down.

'How did you travel to and from the meeting at Mrs Bolton's house?' Palmer fired at her.

'I drove.'

'And approximately,' Barrett's eyes twinkled a little, 'how long would you say it takes you to get to the address?'

'From here, I'd say no more than thirty minutes. Depending on the traffic.'

'And you can't remember the exact time you returned home on that day?'

'Not the exact time.' Pauline was visibly flustered. 'Sometime between seven and eight.'

Palmer and Barrett both knew the time of death was around 7pm, and Pauline didn't have a solid alibi.

'Pauline Robinson, I am arresting you on suspicion of murder …' Barrett stepped closer to Pauline, whose face filled with horror.

'What?' Roger's eyes almost popped out of his head.

'We will be taking you to the station where a formal interview will take place.'

'You can't do this!' Roger's face was puce.

'Sir, please step out of the way.' Palmer towered over the little man who looked like a kettle about to boil.

'She's not done anything wrong.'

'We have evidence to the contrary.' Barrett led the stunned Pauline out of the house and into the back of the car.

'I'll get a solicitor!' Roger called from the doorway, still wearing his slippers, looking enraged. 'Don't say a word until you've been given legal advice.'

As Pauline sat in the back of the car, tears rolled down her cheeks. She couldn't look at Roger as the car pulled away, in case it was the last time she ever saw him, as a free woman.

Rushing back into the house, Roger, with a shaking hand, picked up the telephone and dialled Marion Bolton's landline. When Alfred answered, Roger thought he was going to pass out with relief.

'I need your help.' His breathless words were hurried. 'It's Pauline. She's in trouble.'

'Slow down, Roger.' Alfred held the phone to his ear and spoke calmly.

'The police have arrested her!' Roger squealed.

'What? Why?' Alfred did his best to process the news.

'They think she had something to do with Toni's death.'

Despite not having much in common, the two men often played golf together. Neither minded the other's company and it was handy having a golf buddy who lived close by.

'How can I help?'

'Well, I know this isn't exactly your area, but do you have the number of a good solicitor?'

'Roger, I'm an accountant.' Alfred folded the newspaper he'd been reading and threw it aside.

'But you must know someone? Come on, Alf, I could really do with your help. She's in trouble.'

As it so happened, Alfred did have the number of a trusted solicitor, but before handing over the information he wanted to know a bit more.

'Why have they arrested her? Why do they think she's involved?'

'I don't really know.' Roger scratched his head. 'They were asking her when she last saw Toni, and then what time she came back from book club. When she couldn't give an exact time, they arrested her, but I think there's more to it than that. There's a bit of history with us and Toni.'

'Oh?' Alfred was intrigued.

'Well, we had a bit of a falling out recently.'

'What about?'

'Money. Nothing very serious.' Roger was careful not to give away too much. He knew Marion would find out, if he told Alfred, and if those women were good at anything it was gossiping.

'I do have a pal who might be able to help.' Alfred realised that Roger was not about to implicate his wife in someone's murder, and thought it best not to press the matter. 'He's reliable and knows his stuff, but he's not cheap.'

Great, thought Roger to himself, *why not bleed me of more money I don't have?*

'That's no problem, Alf. We need counsel.'

'It is Sunday though,' Alfred said thoughtfully, wondering if it would be unfair to pass on his friend's mobile number to Roger. While he took a moment to decide what to do, the smell of roast beef came floating in from the kitchen. Marion was busy cooking and he could hear the gentle hum of classical music coming from the radio.

'I can't make any promises, Rog, but let me give him a call and see what I can do. I'll call you back as soon as I can.'

'Thank you.' Roger felt a lump forming in his throat. 'I'm going down to the station. The thought of her being there on her own ...'

'Fine, but take your mobile so that I can get hold of you when I've spoken to my friend.'

'Yes. Good thinking.' Roger started to kick off his slippers. 'I appreciate your help, Alf.'

'Be in touch,' Alfred said, hanging up the phone and following the scent into the kitchen.

'You won't believe this,' Alfred went over to the fridge and started to pour himself a glass of orange juice, 'but Pauline has just been arrested for Toni's murder.'

Marion dropped the wooden spoon she was stirring with and spun round to interrogate her husband.

At the station, Pauline was shown to a cell. She'd never been inside a police station before, let alone locked up in one. Not only was she terrified that she was going to be sent to prison, but her pride had also taken a knock. She was an upstanding citizen, not some ruffian who belonged behind bars. Sitting awkwardly on the squeaky blue mattress, she tried to think. Why were they so quick to arrest her? She wondered if they knew more than they had let on. Racking her brains, Pauline tried to think if there was anything that could link her to the crime. Yes, she had been angry with Toni, but not enough to kill her. A bead of sweat rolled down the back of her neck, making her shiver – like someone had walked over her grave. How could she prove she was innocent? Her mind whirled, around and around, trying to come up with the answer. She knew she wasn't responsible, but that wasn't enough. She'd heard stories of innocent people being sent to prison. What if that happened to her? How would Roger cope on his own? It didn't bear thinking about. They'd been married for thirty-five years and had never spent more than a night apart.

Roger retired from being a teacher when they decided to start the business together. He'd been so enthusiastic about the project and it had put a spring back in his step. She was the brains behind the idea and he was going to be the driver. They thought they had everything worked out, everything except a proper, legally binding agreement with Toni. Pauline had overlooked that aspect because of their friendship, a decision she now bitterly regretted.

After leaving Pauline to sweat for a few hours, Barrett ordered her to be brought to an interview room for questioning. She sat in the chair, looking like a broken woman, and Palmer wondered if she might just confess, saving them all time.

'Pauline.' Barrett cleared his throat and arranged some papers on the table in front of him. 'I would like you to take us through what happened on the evening of June twenty-first.'

Pauline turned and looked at the duty solicitor who sat on her left. The young man gave her a small nod.

'No comment,' she said quietly.

'How long have you known the deceased?'

'No comment.'

'You were friends, weren't you?' Palmer queried.

'You wanted to go into business with her, is that right?' Barrett asked.

Pauline knew then that they knew everything.

'She was going to be your business partner in a mobile library venture, wasn't she?' Barrett's gaze did not falter.

Pauline looked at her solicitor again. He was young enough to be her son.

'Well, if you know everything, then what's the point?' She shrugged and folded her arms.

'I'd say it is a motive for murder.' Palmer leant in.

'I didn't kill her.' Pauline's voice was higher than normal. 'Why would I kill her?'

'Revenge. Money. Plenty of reasons I can think of.' Palmer stroked his chin thoughtfully.

'I'm in my mid-sixties, Detective. I have a bad hip. I am not a killer.' She half laughed, finding the situation almost amusing.

'How did you convince her to meet you on the common? Did you say you wanted to have a talk and work things out?' Barrett asked.

'This is absurd.'

'A woman is dead. Murdered. I would say that absurd isn't quite the right choice of word.' Barrett spoke carefully.

'I have told you, I went home after leaving the book club. I did not go to the common to meet her, or any such thing.' Pauline was beginning to get irritated.

'These are some messages sent between you and Toni. Do you recognise this conversation?' Barrett slid the printed sheets across the table to her.

Pauline ran her eye over them and sighed. 'Yes.'

'It appears that you were threatening Toni Jones.' Barrett sat back in his chair.

Pauline shrugged. 'No comment.'

'What do you think, sir?' Back in the incident room, Palmer was eating a sandwich he'd grabbed when he went to see his son.

'Well, we know she has motive.' Barrett was standing looking at the board. 'But she's no killer. I can't see her stripping the body and planting petals in the hair. It just doesn't fit.'

'I agree.' Palmer brushed some crumbs off his trousers. 'I've asked for the CCTV footage from Huntingdon Road, going in to Bar Hill, from six-thirty onwards. Perhaps that will confirm the time she returned home.'

'Good work. Once you've been through the footage come and get me. I'll be in my office.'

'Sir, because of the way the body was treated, are you sure we shouldn't start thinking it's possible that this is a serial?'

'No, not yet. Let's investigate the facts, Joe, not some hunch.' Barrett growled. 'At the moment we have one body, one crime. Don't get ahead of yourself.'

'Yes, sir. I'll get on to the CCTV right away. The sooner we prove where Pauline was, the better.'

Palmer sat down at his desk and turned on his computer. The screen flashed up telling him he had one new email and he was pleased to see it was from the traffic police. Palmer prepared himself for a very boring hour watching cars on the main road, keeping his eyes peeled for Pauline's car, but after only five minutes he saw what he was looking for. The time on the recording was 6.37pm.

'Bingo.' Palmer leapt out of his seat and knocked on Barrett's door.

'Come in,' Barrett boomed from inside.

'It looks like we will need to release Pauline Robinson, sir. Her car was on Huntingdon Road at six thirty-seven. She couldn't have killed Toni Jones.'

'God damn it.' Barrett slammed down his hands. 'Then our killer is still out there. Back to square one.'

'I'll arrange for Pauline to be released.'

Barrett marched past Palmer and into the incident room. 'We are missing something. I want to speak to Marion Bolton. Get in touch with her and ask her to come in to the station. She knows more than she told us and I want to know exactly what that is.'

Chapter 13

4.40pm 24 June

'So, she's been released.' Marion put down her book and looked across at her husband.

'That's what Roger said.' Alfred was in a pensive mood. 'Hard to believe they arrested her in the first place, I mean, really, at her age, I just can't see it.'

'Yes, and she has that trouble with her hip,' Marion agreed. 'Still they must have had some reason.'

'But she's out now, so that is the end of it.' Alfred was as keen as his wife to know exactly what had gone on, but felt guilty for gossiping, and was not a man who liked to speculate without knowing all the facts.

'Well, I'm not sure what to do. Do I call her and see if she's alright? Do I leave her alone? It's all so complicated.' Marion rubbed her temples.

'I think you need to try and stop involving yourself.' Alfred went and sat next to his wife. 'The shock of Toni's death is still so raw. You all need time to process it. She may not have been everyone's cup of tea, but she didn't deserve to end her days like that.'

'The book club hasn't been the same for a while. It used to be fun and light-hearted but it's got so serious, and all these different women just can't seem to get along. I'm tired of it.'

'Then stop doing it.' Alfred put his arm around Marion. 'You don't need this stress.' He kissed her forehead. 'It's not worth it.'

'Maybe you're right. I just need to step back. They're all at it – Shirley, Amy, Janet, all fighting and bitching. I don't know where it went wrong. Honestly, you'd think there was nothing more harmless than a book club.' She sighed and stroked the cover of her book with her hand.

'I was thinking—' Alfred was determined to lift his wife's spirit. 'What if we took the motorhome and went away for a while? Just the two of us. We could go and explore Holland. You've always wanted to do that.'

Marion's eyes filled with tears. 'You're so good to me. I do love you, you old bugger.'

'Less of the old, missy,' he said, as the phone rang.

'I'll get it.' Marion stood.

'Hello? The Bolton residence.' Alfred watched as her face fell. 'Oh, hello, Inspector.' He knew in that moment there was no way they could leave the country now. 'Yes,' Marion spoke down the phone, 'yes, I'll come in tomorrow morning. Okay, yes, see you at ten o'clock. Okay. Goodbye.' She hung up and closed her eyes. 'They want me to go to the station and give them a formal statement tomorrow. When will this ever end?'

Alfred embraced his wife, knowing it would only be over when the person responsible was safely behind bars.

*

Across town, both Shirley and Janet were preparing to leave work. Shirley filled in the forms she needed to before walking out of the care home and getting into her car. She sat there for a while, resting her head on the steering wheel, wishing that her life was different.

But Janet was not the same as her friend. She didn't wish for bigger and better things, she was content with her lot. As long as she had a good book on the go, that was all that mattered.

She locked up the shop and entered the alleyway to the side, which led to the stairs up to her flat. She was thankful that her Sunday had been quiet. Often, she had to contend with drunk, grumpy punters who had just blown their monthly income on backing the wrong horse, but that day had been blissfully easy, apart from her conversation with Pauline.

As Janet walked into her gloomy living room she contemplated the information she'd learnt that day. She knew only too well how people could go to pieces over money, and felt herself briefly pitying Pauline. The pity didn't last long, though, and, as she made herself some packet noodles on the stove, she decided to call Shirley for a chat.

'Hi.' Shirley's tone was unusually flat and Janet felt like she'd made a mistake by calling.

'You OK?' she asked tentatively.

'Yeah, just fed up. What you up to?'

'Thought I'd call for a chat. I saw Pauline today.' She dangled the carrot for her friend.

'Oh yeah?' Shirley had no intention of biting.

'She came into the bookies.' Janet was determined to have her fun with this.

'Bit odd.' Shirley's ears had pricked up. 'How come?'

'I thought you'd never ask,' Janet sniggered. 'She came to place a bet.'

'No way!'

'Yes, way, and you'll never guess what ...' Janet paused to increase the tension, 'she was in debt because of Toni.' Shirley was silent and Janet wondered if the line had cut out. 'Are you there?'

'Yeah, sorry, just taking it all in.'

'They were going to start a business together. Some sort of mobile library, or something.'

'Sounds boring.'

'Yes, but with Kindles instead.'

'Sounds even worse!' Shirley cackled.

'Well, Pauline has got herself into serious financial trouble,' Janet tutted, enjoying the gossip.

'How much you talking?'

'Tens of thousands.'

'Holy crap.' Shirley had forgotten all about feeling sorry for herself. The conversation had cheered her up no end. There was sometimes nothing better than realising that other people were also struggling. 'Well, she kept that to herself.'

'You would, though, wouldn't you,' Janet mused, 'if your so-called business partner showed up dead after screwing you over.'

'You don't think …' Shirley held her breath.

'I'm not saying that, but it doesn't look good for her, does it?' Janet smiled and plunged a mouthful of tepid noodles into her mouth, chewing thoughtfully. 'You got any plans tonight?'

'I've just finished work. I'm sitting in the car park.' The wave of melancholy came back and hit Shirley in the chest.

'I'm staying in, if you want to come over? We could watch TV, or something.' Janet was facing another quiet, lonely night in.

'Kayla's at home. She needs dinner.' Shirley dreaded returning to her house and wished she could accept Janet's invitation. 'Another time, yeah?'

'Sure.' Her disappointment rang through the word.

'Right, well, I can't sit here all day. I'd better get going. Speak soon.' And with that, Shirley hung up.

Janet sat in the dim room, looking down at her bowl of cold, soggy noodles. She didn't normally feel sorry for herself but, on this occasion, she felt let down. She'd been trying to do Shirley a favour and cheer her up, but as was typical of their friendship, it was a one-way street.

Fed up of being let down by Shirley, Janet decided she wouldn't sit and sulk, and would instead take herself out of the crappy flat and go for a walk. The weather had perked up and blue sky was beginning to break through.

Pulling the door closed behind her and locking it, Janet lifted her face towards the warm sunshine. She felt better already.

With her mobile phone in her pocket, she put in her headphones and started to listen to an audio book she'd recently downloaded on Shirley's recommendation. It was a domestic noir, which was just the sort of thing Janet enjoyed reading. The book started off well and the narrator pulled her in as she walked along, enjoying herself and feeling less alone.

It didn't take Janet long to make her way to Stourbridge Common. She didn't know why, but she felt drawn to it and had always enjoyed walking along the river. That early evening, the river was busy with boats, and people sitting on the grass enjoying cans of cider. Janet suspected most of them were students – although the city got quieter in the summer because many students returned home, some stayed to work and continued to party. It was a nice place to live, much nicer than the place in Kent, near Dartford, where Janet had been raised with her four brothers and two sisters. Her mother, like her, was a single parent, and had suffered from a serious drug problem.

When she was a schoolgirl, Janet had been on a trip to Cambridge and had decided that somehow, one day, she would live there. By the time she was old enough to leave school, she'd fled from her troubled family home and managed to get work in the city as a cleaner in a pub. Not long after that she'd fallen pregnant with Dean.

As Janet continued walking along the path by the river, she soon found herself at the spot where Toni's body had been discovered. Bunches of flowers and cuddly toys lay in a row, looking tired after being battered by the elements. Janet wondered who all the people were who'd left flowers, so she bent down to read some of the notes attached. It wasn't the grand memorial Toni would have wanted, Janet knew that much.

While she was inspecting the flowers, a shadow cast over her and she spun around, terrified, to find Gerald standing behind her.

She recognised him from the pictures in the press, but they'd never met in person.

His face was pale and awash with tears. Janet stood and moved aside so he could get a better look at the flowers and soft toys.

'I'm sorry for your loss.' She swallowed.

'Thank you,' Gerald responded, with robotic precision.

'I'm Janet. I knew your wife.'

'Knew her?' Gerald turned to face the stranger. 'How?'

'I'm a member of the book club.' Janet didn't know why she was telling him this, but she felt compelled to be honest.

'You saw her that night?' Janet noticed that Gerald was holding a garden gnome in his arms.

'Yes, I did.' Janet scratched her neck nervously. Eczema was irritating her skin.

Gerald turned his attention back to the ratty bunches of flowers. 'I wanted to leave something that would last,' he said, giving the gnome pride of place among the offerings. 'Flowers die, don't they.' He removed a handkerchief from his pocket and blew his nose.

Janet stood awkwardly, not knowing what to say. She wasn't comfortable with shows of affection, especially with men she didn't know, but she wanted him to know that she was sorry.

'Are the police getting anywhere with their investigation?' she asked tenderly.

Gerald stiffened. 'They thought I might be responsible.' He shook his head with disgust. 'I could never ...' his words trailed off.

'I'm sure they were just covering every possibility.' Janet blushed and looked at the ground. She was wearing her tatty old Birkenstock style sandals and her toenails were long and grubby looking. She made a mental note to trim them when she got home.

'How long had you known my wife?'

'We weren't close. More like acquaintances.' Janet didn't see the point in lying to the man.

'How did she seem at the book club that day?' The poor man wanted answers so badly, it showed all over his face, but Janet wasn't in a position to help.

'Her normal self.' She shrugged, not wanting to mention the sniping that had taken place at the meeting. Feeling like the conversation was going somewhere she'd rather it didn't, Janet looked down at her old Casio wristwatch. 'I'd better be going.'

'Yes, of course.' Gerald was on his haunches, cupping the gnome in his hands as if it were a baby.

'It was nice to meet you.' She turned and hurried away, feeling like she couldn't breathe.

*

The steak sizzled in the pan, filling the room with a meaty smoke, as Amy stood over the hob, basting the sirloins with copious amounts of butter. Since she'd fallen pregnant she'd had a craving for red meat. Luckily, her husband, Johnny, shared her passion and was only too happy to let her cook what she pleased.

He was exhausted, but pleased to be home. Since he'd learnt about the murder, he'd wanted to come back to his wife. He didn't like the idea of her being alone in the house, especially since the victim was one of her friends.

He removed the cork from a bottle of Rioja as he hummed along to the rock song that was playing on the radio. Johnny was not Cambridge born and bred, but when his wife had proposed that they should leave London, he was happy enough to go along with it. He didn't have the sort of job that required him to be in an office from 9am until 5pm, and the commute to London was easy – on the occasions he was needed there.

'It's hard to believe someone we know has been murdered. Makes you thankful for every moment you have.' Amy stood, turning the asparagus over in the griddle pan while the steaks rested. Johnny poured himself a glass of wine and went over to his wife, wrapping his arms around her bump and holding their child in his hands.

'We are so lucky.' He kissed her neck. 'I don't know what I'd do without you.'

'Spend more time playing sport or in the pub with your friends, I suspect.' She elbowed him playfully in the ribs.

'How's that husband of hers doing? What's his name?'

'Gerald. I don't know. It's difficult really. I knew her but we stopped being friends a long time ago. I'm not sure what went wrong, I just think we clashed in the end. I used to have a lot of time for her.'

'Yes, I remember.' Johnny took a swig of his red wine.

'Eww, you know I can't stand the smell at the moment!' She put her hand over her mouth and nose in an exaggerated fashion and made a face.

'Sorry!' He backed away, holding up his hands in a conciliatory move.

'It's OK, really.' She waved a tea towel in his direction before bending to check the chips in the oven. 'Lay the table, will you?'

Minutes later their dinner was ready and they sat down to enjoy the expensive meat.

'The nursery is really coming along,' she said, savouring the flavour of the food, which seemed heightened somehow by being pregnant. 'You know, I'm sure it's a boy.' Amy rested her hand on her tummy. 'All this red meat, it must be! A mini Johnny, now there is a thought.' She twisted her hair into a knot on her head and pinned it up. 'Hot in here tonight,' she said, fanning herself with a napkin.

'The temperature isn't the only thing …' Johnny leant across the table and raised his eyebrows up and down.

Throwing back her head she laughed and tossed the napkin at him. 'Honestly, I heard better chat up lines when I was a teenager!'

'It's good to see you laughing.' Johnny sat back in his chair, content that he'd achieved his goal.

'I've not been that bad.' Amy frowned.

'No, but you've had a lot on. I'm sorry I've been working away so much. This job is the last one for a while. I promise.'

'Someone has to pay the mortgage on this place.' It was his turn to frown.

'You're not worried about money, are you?'

'No, but I do wonder what it will be like when mini Johnny arrives and you have to go away.'

'That's the whole reason I'm working so hard at the moment, so it doesn't have to happen.' Johnny was tired and the last thing he wanted was *that* conversation again.

'You'd rather I didn't miss you?' He could see Amy was getting emotional, and he understood her point, but he'd only been home for a few hours and had been hoping to have a nice dinner with his wife. That prospect was looking less and less likely.

'Amy, please, can we just enjoy dinner? We'll talk about this tomorrow.' He took another sip of wine, enjoying the warm, fruity flavour that trickled down his throat.

'Sure.' She threw her cutlery down on the table. 'You decide. You call all the shots. I'll just sit here like the little wife and never open my mouth.' Her face was flushed and Johnny knew there was no escaping an argument now. Rubbing his face with his hands he let out a long sigh.

'Oh, I'm sorry.' She got to her feet, the tears welling in her eyes. 'You just seem to think that everything is the same, but it isn't. You cheated on me. I can't just forget that.'

'I told you, it was a one-night-stand. I've admitted it, and I've said I'm sorry until I'm blue in the face. What more do you want? What else can I do?'

'I think you've done enough already.' She patted her bump, soothing the child growing inside her, which was beginning to kick her ribs. The child could sense her upset, she knew it.

'Come on, babe, just sit down and finish this lovely steak.'

'I've lost my appetite,' she said – and she had. 'I'm going upstairs to have a shower. You can clean up this mess.' Amy left the room wondering if the real mess could ever really be cleared up at all.

Chapter 14

5.50am 25 June

As was usual at that time of year, Midsummer Common had been host to the Midsummer Fair, in which hordes of travellers in caravans descended and set up stalls to sell their wares. The city had been subjected to an exhausting weekend and fireworks, set off by various universities, had echoed around the sky late into the night.

A group of late-night revellers were returning home, still dressed in the clothes they had been wearing the night before, and stumbled, worse for wear, along the path that followed the river towards Magdalene Bridge. The young men, some of whom were still sipping from beer cans, joked and laughed about the night's activities, followed sheepishly by young women whose make-up had made its way down their faces. Dressed in their weekend best, the girls tottered along in their heels, trying to keep up, while their feet throbbed.

On the river, a few ducks and a pair of swans were gliding elegantly upstream, unaware of the gaggle walking alongside them.

As the group got closer to the bridge, one of the young women noticed something in the water, wedged between two punts. As she stopped walking and took a few steps closer, she lost her footing on the riverbank and ended up on her bottom. The grass was wet with dew and her bare legs did not approve of the sensation. Laughing, one of the men extended a hand to help her up.

'What's that?' She pointed with her chipped, red painted nail.

He heaved the woman back up to her feet, which was no easy task considering neither of them had slept and she was determined to keep her heels on, and craned his neck to get a better look.

'Holy crap.' He stepped back. 'Rob, come and have a look at this. It's a body in the water.'

One of the women began to scream. 'Do something, get her out!' But another of the young men appeared and pointed out that the body was lying face down in the water and was bloated. The person was clearly dead.

'It's too late,' one of the men, who was a medical student, confirmed. 'Look at the state of her. We need to call the police.'

Within fifteen minutes the emergency services were at the scene. The girls, who were all shivering with shock, had been given foil blankets and were being comforted by ambulance workers, while the police cordoned off the area with crime scene tape. The young men stood, pale-faced, some of them smoking roll-ups, looking far less cocky than they had done twenty minutes earlier. This was not how any of them had expected to end their year at university.

It took a little while for the dive team to arrive and start making preparations to remove the body from the water, and before they did that, the group who had made the discovery were whisked away, and a tent was erected in which the body would be examined.

The divers entered the cold, still water in wetsuits, and proceeded to put bags over the head, hands and feet to preserve any evidence. It wasn't clear whether the body was that of a murder victim, or some unfortunate soul who had fallen into the river and drowned by accident. But all the services involved thought the latter unlikely: the river was not fast moving, or deep, so it seemed improbable that this was misadventure.

The police and forensic teams knew the city would be waking up and they needed to act quickly. It was their job to protect the public from having to see such unpleasant things.

Once the body was in the tent, the dead woman was laid out on her back. Her face, wrapped in a plastic bag, was distorted, and straggles of long hair were snaked around her throat. From the state of her body it was clear she had been dead for some hours.

What wasn't clear at that stage, was how she had ended up in the river in the first place.

DI Palmer arrived at the scene tired and hungry.

'Looks like you've got your hands full at the moment,' the crime scene investigator said, looking down at the body.

'Tell me about this one.' Palmer let out a tired breath.

'She's been in the water for some time. Probably since nine or ten o'clock last night. I'll need to do a more extensive examination, but it appears that she has a fractured skull.'

Palmer leant down to get a closer look at the body. 'I don't know how you boys can tell that. Apart from being dead, she looks in good nick, to me.'

'That's why I'm in forensics and you're a copper,' the man laughed.

'I can't say at this stage what caused the fracture – whether it's as the result of a blow to the head, or from a fall. I also can't be certain if that is what killed her, until I get her back to the lab.' The technician bent down and carefully removed some of the hair from around the woman's neck. 'And, see here, these marks on her neck …' The statement was self-explanatory.

'Give me something more,' Palmer pleaded.

'How about this?' The forensic investigator held up a bag containing a soaking wet purse. 'We found it in the deceased's pocket.'

'Bingo!' Palmer clapped his gloved hands together. 'We have a name.'

'We do. She might look like she was homeless, but my bet is that this belongs to her. She also had a mobile phone in her pocket. We'll do our best to retrieve everything that was on it.'

'If you had to hazard a guess?' Palmer was not going to let his colleague off the hook.

'I'd say misadventure is unlikely. She looks too old to be a student, mucking about on the river, besides, why has no one reported it? Either she ended up falling off a bridge, alone, or someone did this to her. My professional opinion is the latter.'

Palmer nodded gravely. 'That's what I thought. Send the report over as soon as you have it. I need to start looking at CCTV. The joys of the job.' Palmer left the tent, dreading the day ahead.

*

At precisely 7.32am, Shirley's mobile phone rang, waking her from her slumber. Daylight poured in through the cheap, thin curtains and she squinted against the bright light, fumbling on her bedside table for the phone. Before checking the name on the screen, she picked up, irritated at being woken.

'Yes,' her hoarse, sleepy voice travelled down the line.

'Shirl, it's Dean, 'ave you seen Mum?' The young man could tell that he'd woken his mother's friend, but felt no reason to apologise.

'Dean. Why are you calling me at this time?' She rolled over onto her back, clutching the phone to her ear, aware that Grant, her husband, had not come to bed.

'She ain't here.'

'So?' Shirley groaned, rolling onto her side again and shutting her eyes.

'She should be 'ere.' Dean spoke like all the other hood-rats in his area, and his distinct lack of manners, which was something he shared with his mother, did not endear him to Shirley, especially at that time of the morning. 'It's me birthday.'

'Oh.' Shirley sat up in bed, rubbing her eyes. 'Sorry, Dean, but what has that got to do with anything?'

'She's always awake first when it's me birthday. She sets me presents out and then we go to Macca's for brekkie. Been like that every year, but I don't know where she is and she ain't answerin' her phone neither.'

Shirley let out a sigh. 'Maybe she thought a takeaway breakfast would make a change, or something?'

'Nah. And she ain't slept in her bed.' Dean, who normally sounded so sure of himself, suddenly sounded like a frightened little boy.

'Well, I'm sorry you can't get hold of her, but I can't help.' Shirley did not want to have been woken up by this.

'Alright.' Dean sounded huffy. 'Just thought maybe you could 'elp.'

'If I could, I would,' Shirley replied gruffly. 'Now, if you don't mind, I'd like to go back to sleep.'

'See ya, then.'

'Happy birthday,' Shirley managed to say brightly before he'd hung up the phone. *That boy is a little sh*it, she thought to herself as she thumped her pillow into shape and tried to get back to sleep.

Outside, the birds were singing and the sound of the bin lorry was growing ever closer. Shirley tossed and turned, burying her face in the pillow, which was slightly damp from the sweat she'd secreted during her sleep. She didn't sleep so well these days, and hadn't for some months.

Shirley was grateful that she had a late shift at work that day, as she'd planned on having a lie in. These days, Kayla insisted on walking herself to school, and had made it clear that she wouldn't be seen dead with her mother. For a while Shirley had persisted in waking up her daughter, making her breakfast, and helping her get ready for school, but ever since puberty had struck, Kayla had become even more difficult than before. Rather than fight it, Shirley had decided to let her get on with it, and tried to keep out of her way, avoiding confrontation wherever possible.

When the music came blaring from Kayla's room, Shirley gave up trying to sleep, and sat up in bed to take a sip from the tepid water in the glass next to her bed. Always part of her routine, she turned on the radio to catch the news and find some happy music to encourage her to get up. After listening to Taylor Swift strangle a cat, she turned up the volume ready to catch the headlines.

'Welcome to the eight o'clock news. Our headlines today: a body has been discovered in the River Cam, in Cambridge city centre. The female was discovered by students returning home after a party, in the early hours of this morning. The police have not yet confirmed the cause of death, or the identity of the woman, but are asking members of the public who may have seen something, to come forward. In other news …'

She swung her chunky legs out of the bed and sat on the side, looking out of the crack in the curtains. The world was waking up and she watched as the bin men crashed around emptying bins into the truck. Shirley was initially extremely irritated when Dean had called, but sitting there, having heard the news, she could feel a ball of tension forming in her stomach. Telling herself that it was just a result of the kebab she'd eaten the night before, she got up and went for a shower. Something had to help drown out the noise that was coming from her daughter's bedroom and the feeling of sickness in her stomach, and the pressure of the water might just do it.

*

Back at Parkside police station, DI Palmer was sitting in his seat, clicking a biro furiously, while he waited for DCI Barrett to appear. There had been a significant development with the Toni Jones case, and he couldn't wait to break the news to his boss, who had been foul-tempered the past few days.

Palmer knew the DCI was often pricklier during the summer months. He'd lost his wife to cancer in July, three years ago, and he was always affected during the weeks leading up to her anniversary. Barrett had never talked about losing his wife, but everyone who knew him knew what a difficult time it had been for him, and could see that it still took its toll on him emotionally.

When Barrett appeared, having spent his first night at home since the discovery of Toni's body, Palmer flew out of his chair and bounded towards him like an overzealous puppy.

'Sir, there has been a huge development with the case.' Palmer was nearly breathless with excitement.

'At least let me get in the door, Joe.' Barrett smiled for the first time since Palmer could remember.

'This morning, the body of a woman was discovered in the river, close to Bridge Street.'

'Yes, yes,' Barrett said impatiently, 'I know all this.'

'The CSI is sure she has a fractured skull, and there were marks around her neck that look like bruising.' Barrett raised his eyebrows.

'And?'

'And a purse was found on the victim.' Palmer was enjoying his brief moment of power.

'Get on with it.' Barrett's amusement at the situation was waning.

'We believe the victim was a Miss Janet Cox.' Palmer watched with glee as the information was processed by Barrett.

'You mean, Janet Cox who attended the book club with Toni Jones?'

'We think so, sir.'

Barrett nodded, and walked over to the wall that displayed all the information they had gathered about the victim.

'You said she was found in the water, was she naked?'

'No, sir, she was clothed.'

'Any sign of petals?'

'No, sir.' Palmer resented having to admit that.

'Two women, who were members of the same book club, are dead within three days of each other.' Palmer didn't interrupt. He knew better than to cut in when the cogs of his boss's mind were hard at work. Palmer sat quietly, a few chairs away, and waited, knowing instructions would be given soon.

Despite Barrett occasionally being difficult to work with, Palmer had the upmost respect for his superior, and never failed to be impressed by the diligence the man showed with every case.

Barrett stood slowly and cleared his throat, resulting in the room falling instantly silent.

'I want every single woman who was at that book meeting interviewed immediately. I want to know about their financial situations, their marriages, their children, and their careers. Hell, I want to know their inside leg measurements.' Palmer stifled a smirk. 'We go back to basics and start this investigation with new eyes. Somehow, the book club is the link.'

'Sir,' Palmer spoke solemnly, 'is this not now a serial case?'

'The victims are linked, yes,' Barrett walked backwards and forwards, thinking, 'but we don't know that the killer is. Leave no stone unturned. Double-check every damn piece of information any of those women give you. Someone knows something, and my guess is that one of them is lying.'

'Sir, Marion Bolton is expected to arrive for an interview at ten.' Palmer looked up at the clock on the wall, which told them it was 8.30am.

'Good. We'll start with her.' Barrett slipped off his jacket, already feeling the heat from the unusually hot June weather, to signify to the rest of the room that he was definitely ready for work. 'The rest, I don't care if they are sitting at the bedside of their dying parents, you haul them in here and dig deep. Palmer,' he called across the room, 'I want the forensic report as soon as it comes in.'

'Yes, sir.'

'Today, ladies and gents, we break this case.' His speech was old fashioned and clichéd but it always rallied the troops. They all wanted justice for the victims, but keeping Barrett happy was even more important to some of them, and, being the cantankerous, stubborn man that he was, he didn't care how the results came, as long as they got them.

Chapter 15

10am 25 June

Marion arrived at the police station at precisely ten o'clock. She was dressed in her Sunday best and looked as if she might have just come from church.

She sat stiffly on a plastic chair opposite the reception desk, waiting for Barrett to call her in. Alfred was perched beside her, holding her hand. The couple, who were both close to pension age, looked very out of place. Neither had yet heard that another body had been discovered, let alone that the body belonged to Janet Cox.

Barrett arrived with his sleeves rolled up, followed by Palmer, and ushered the nervous couple out of reception and towards an interview room. His manner was cooler than it had been previously, and Marion and Alfred both noticed the difference.

'Tea?' Barrett asked, out of habit rather than politeness.

'Not for me.' Marion had to stop herself from calling him pet. Alfred shook his head and the four of them took their seats in the small, stuffy room.

'You have no windows in here,' Alfred commented, looking around at the pale blue walls.

'Very observant, Mr Bolton.' Barrett was not in the mood for small talk, and he made sure the people sitting opposite him knew that. Alfred, who looked somewhat put out, folded his arms across his chest and looked to his wife.

'You are not under arrest.' Palmer did his best to make Marion feel at home. He appreciated his boss's desire to get to the truth, but couldn't abide some of his methods.

'We need to know everything you know about Toni Jones, Mrs Bolton.' He fixed the aging woman with a stare. 'Absolutely everything.'

'I've told you all about the night she went missing.' Marion looked decidedly distressed.

'I'm interested in some details about her personal life,' Barrett said, noticing the look that passed between the husband and wife. Still, Marion sat in silence.

'Are you aware that another body has been discovered in the city this morning?'

Their reaction suggested they were not aware, and that this was the first time they had heard the news.

'The recent victim has links to Toni Jones.' Barrett wasn't ready to name Janet until the identification had been confirmed and the next of kin had been informed.

'Oh!' Marion's wrinkled hand went up to her quivering lip. 'Who?'

'I am not at liberty to divulge that information at this time.' Barrett wore his best poker face. 'I would like to ask you again about the reputed affair Toni Jones had.'

Marion's face stiffened, and beneath the table her husband's hand found her knee and rested there.

'We have reason to believe that the personal life of the victim may be linked to the motive for her murder. I urge you,' he leant across the table, softening his tone, 'to tell me anything you know.'

Still, Marion remained tight-lipped, although Barrett couldn't tell if she was being bloody-minded or she was frightened.

'Mrs Bolton.' It was Palmer's turn to have a go at breaking her down. 'You will not be in trouble.'

'But holding back information that might be vital to a murder investigation,' Barrett cut in, embracing his role as bad cop, 'is a criminal offence.'

Marion looked at Alfred again and the detectives watched him offer her an approving nod.

'It's not my place to destroy people's marriages.' Marion's twinkling eyes filled with tears. Palmer and Barrett both knew when to shut up and they waited patiently for the woman to tell them what she knew.

'It's alright, love. You can tell them,' Alfred encouraged, smiling kindly. 'He was a married man,' Marion hissed at her husband.

'Who was?' Barrett pressed.

'Grant.' Marion hung her head and put her face in her hands. 'Grant Grubb.'

Alfred, who watched the reaction of both policemen closely, nodded in support of his wife. 'It's true,' the old man added, 'Marion told me a few years ago when she found out.'

'What was I supposed to do?' Marion sniffed, reaching for a hankie that was in her bag. 'It wasn't my place to tell.' Her bottom lip straightened and she regained her composure.

'How did you discover the affair?'

Again, Marion and Alfred shared a look. 'You might as well tell them everything, love.'

Marion looked across at Barrett, who made it clear he was waiting for a proper explanation, and let out a long, tired sigh.

'Very well.' She put her hands in her lap and straightened her back. 'I found out soon after it began. I'd met Toni on an online book club. She was a character, I liked her, and when we realised we lived close by, we met up. I used to have coffee with her and discuss books. She was an interesting woman. Not what I'd call worldly,' Barrett wondered what Marion considered to be 'worldly', 'but she were curious about the world and had a passion for literature. We got on well enough and enjoyed each other's company. Well, anyway, she told me she'd met a chap and that she were considering having an affair. I said "don't be daft, you've got a good man", but she said he was very persuasive. Anyway, next thing I knew, her marriage to Mike had ended. I only met Mike once, lovely man, and I was sad for her when the marriage fell apart. One afternoon, when we were chatting online, she confessed. Said that this Grant had been a mistake, but that it was too late and Mike had found out. I didn't know nowt about how he found out, all I know is that it was the end of the marriage. Toni was actually so upset she stopped seeing Grant. A few months later she'd met Gerald, and soon after they were married. I didn't think anything of it until Shirley joined the book club.' Marion's shoulders dropped with despair. 'It became obvious when we had our book club Christmas party, and Shirley showed up with her husband. I was daft and hadn't put two and two together at first, but Toni acted very strange all evening, and the next time I saw her she told me that Shirley's Grant was *the* Grant. I was flabbergasted. It was clear to me that Shirley had no idea, so I told Toni to forget about it and move on with her life.' Marion looked like she might draw breath, but didn't, and Palmer scribbled like a man possessed as her verbal diarrhoea was expelled. 'I have to say I found it quite uncomfortable being in Gerald's presence after that. He and Alfred play golf together, don't you, love?' she looked briefly at her husband, who nodded, 'and so whenever he was at the house, I made my excuses. But all this happened so long ago. Toni hadn't said another word about it in all these years, so I didn't think you needed to know.'

'Mrs Bolton, do you think you might be able to recall some slightly more specific dates?' Palmer wasn't hopeful.

'Oh, pet.' She looked briefly embarrassed, before ignoring her slip up and quickly moving on. 'It was so long ago. I really don't think this has anything to do with her death.'

'I think you'll find that is a matter for us to decide.' Barrett showed little tolerance.

'Well, I mean, Grant and Shirley, they seem happy enough to me. I've known men with wandering eyes in my life. Not my Alfred, I mean,' she said, patting her husband's arm. 'But usually they grow out of it. It sounded to me like Grant was immature. But people change.' Neither detective could be sure whether she had said this for their benefit or her own. 'I can't stand the idea of Grant and Shirley having their marriage wrecked for something that is in the past. It just wouldn't be right. What's done is done. Water under the bridge and all that.'

Palmer chewed his lip, wondering if she meant it.

'Do you think Grant Grubb was aware you knew about the affair? Did anyone else know about the affair?'

'Well, Mike knew.' Marion felt like she'd accidently put Mike right in the firing line, and stopped abruptly.

'He knew the identity of the man his wife had been sleeping with?' Barrett pressed.

'You'd have to ask him to be sure.' Marion had said enough and saw no reason to speculate, or frame someone she considered to have had nothing to do with Toni's death. 'Mike's a happily married man now, as far as I know.'

Realising they had got the information they had wanted from Marion, Barrett brought an end to the interview.

'Well, Mr and Mrs Bolton,' he said, standing to signal that the interrogation was over, 'I'd like to thank you for your time today. If we need anything further, an officer will be in touch.'

Not used to being dismissed like small children, the Boltons stood and, guided by Palmer, shuffled out of the interview room.

*

Elly Hale was relieved to see Barrett and Palmer when they reappeared in the incident room.

'Sir, we've had information from forensics. They have confirmed that the victim did have a fractured skull, as a result of blunt force trauma, when she went into the water. There was also water in her lungs, so they know she was still alive when she went into the river. They are doing further tests and will keep us up to date as soon as they know any more. The pathologist says that from the appearance of the injury, she was hit with something. Hard. Repeatedly.'

'Just like Toni Jones.' Palmer mused.

'Yes, but according to the report, the injuries did not break the skin and there was no blood on the victim or around the contusions.' Elly looked pale as she read the clinical notes.

'What about the marks on the neck?' Barrett asked.

'Well, there is bruising, but it is apparently light. No official post-mortem can take place until the Home Office pathologist has arrived though.'

'Where are we with interviewing the other women from the book club?' Barrett walked up to the white board and wrote the name Grant Grubb in large black capitals, before circling it three times.

'It has come to light,' he said, turning to address the room, 'that Mr Grubb, who is the husband of Shirley, a regular at the book club, was the man who had an affair with Toni Jones, which resulted in the break-up of her first marriage. We need to speak to Grant as a matter of urgency. Elly,' he pointed at her, 'I want you to bring him in.' Elly nodded enthusiastically and left the room with her instructions. 'Right, people, we now have two victims with similar wounds who had links to one another. This is no longer a single murder investigation.'

Palmer, who had always been expecting another body to show up, refrained from looking pleased with himself. Being right wasn't always that rewarding.

'We need to inform the next of kin. Palmer and I will visit the victim's home, along with SOCOs. So far, we know that Janet Cox lived with her teenage son in a flat on Milton Road. She worked in the bookmakers below the flat. We interview the son, her colleagues, people who might have seen her yesterday. You,' Barrett pointed to a slightly overweight sergeant, 'get on to the CCTV. See if we can work out where she went into the river. My guess is that it wasn't where we found her.' The chubby man nodded and spun round to face his computer.

'What about the press, sir?' Palmer knew it was a concern and that they would interfere with the investigation.

'Until we've spoken to the son,' Barrett looked at his notes, 'Dean Cox, we keep a lid on it. Nothing leaves this room. Understand?' Everyone gave exaggerated nods. 'To work,' the DCI barked, jolting his team into action.

'Sir,' Palmer spoke quietly, 'what about the wife, Shirley?'

'Her feelings are not my concern at this moment. Let's speak to Grubb and see what he has to say. His wife was at the book club on the night of Toni's murder, so we should talk to her too.'

'Grant has a window cleaning company. I'll call him and tell him to come down to the station.' Palmer approached one of the empty desks and picked up the phone.'

'Tell him we want to speak to him now. Call Elly back. She can go with you to speak to the son.' Palmer grimaced and put down the phone; he hated that part of the job.

'I'll call Grubb.' Barrett put out his hand, waiting for the piece of paper that had the number written on it, which Palmer reluctantly handed over before removing his jacket from the back of a chair and heading downstairs to catch Elly before she left the station.

*

At 11.30am Grant Grubb appeared at Parkside station. He was wearing his work clothes, which included a T-shirt with 'Grant does Windows' written on it. *Not very catchy*, Barrett thought to himself as he showed the nervous looking man into the same interview room that the Boltons had been in earlier that morning.

'Take a seat, Mr Grubb.' Barrett leant against the wall with his hands behind his back, knowing the position of his body would assert authority.

'Do I need a brief?' Grant rubbed his sweaty neck with one of his large, rough hands.

'That is for you to decide. You are not under arrest ... currently.' Barrett watched as Grant swallowed hard, his Adam's apple bobbing up and down like a golf ball in his throat.

'I'm not really sure why I'm 'ere.' His thick Cambridgeshire accent grated on Barrett and DS Singh – who was also participating in the interview.

'We want to talk to you about your relationship with Toni Jones.' Barrett spoke calmly, never taking his eyes off Grant.

'Didn't really know her.' Grant folded his arms across his broad chest.

'That's not what we've heard, Mr Grubb.'

'Oh?' Grant shrugged and looked down at his filthy nails.

'We understand that you had an affair with Mrs Jones, around the time her first marriage ended.'

Grant sat, button-lipped.

'I understand that this is a delicate situation, Mr Grubb, but if you don't want to cooperate, perhaps we should speak to your wife?'

Grant's eyes bulged and he shook his head.

'No, not my missus. She don't know about it. You can't.' Singh moved his chair back a few inches: the man opposite him stank of stale body odour, and he wondered when that T-shirt had last been washed.

'Mr Grubb.' Barrett pulled out a chair and sat down, instantly regretting his move due to the stench that was coming from the man opposite. Singh could see from Barrett's face that he too wished the room had a window. 'I am not interested in harming your marriage, I simply want to know the details of your alleged affair with Toni Jones. It is better for you in the long run if you tell us what you know.'

Grant sat and looked from Singh to Barrett while he contemplated his position.

'What do you want to know exactly?'

'When the affair started, how long it lasted, why it ended.' Barrett reeled off the list, frustrated by the man's stupidity. 'How about you start with where you first met?' Barrett's patience was wearing thin.

'Must have been about four, or four and a half years ago. I used to run, jog like, around the town. Still do sometimes. Anyway, I was runnin' on Jesus Green, just mindin' my own business. All of a sudden, this dog comes up to me and starts barkin' and tryin' to nip at my heels. I weren't that bothered, skinny little thing it was, but the owner, well, she was well embarrassed. I stopped joggin' so that she could come and collect her little dog, which by then had decided I was too big for it to carry on trying to attack.'

'What type was the dog?'

'I dunno. Might have been a boy or a girl.' Grant shrugged.

'No,' Barrett sighed, 'I mean, what type of dog was it? What *breed* was it?'

'Oh, I getcha.' Grant scratched his head. 'Terrier type thing, I think. Sort of sandy-brown colour.' Barrett nodded and made notes. 'Anyway, the owner was Toni. I'd not met her before but she looked nice. Pretty like. Good tits.' Grant laughed, and Singh showed he clearly disliked the description by curling his lip. 'So, she said she was real sorry for what her dog had done, and offered to buy me a drink. I wasn't about to say no to a pretty woman, so I said we should go to the pub on the river, you know, the Fort St George. Good boozer.' Barrett did know it, as did Singh. 'Well, anyway, we had a drink and she was flirtin' with me something awful. Hand on my thigh, asking me where I worked out, all that sort of stuff.'

'Did you know she was married?' Singh asked.

'The ring on her finger told me she was, yeah.'

'We sat for a while, that little dog of hers was on the lead, tied up to the table, and I kept givin' it crisps to keep it quiet and happy.'

'Did you tell her you were married?' Singh continued.

'Now why would I do a thing like that?' Grant threw back his head and gave a loud chuckle. 'An attractive woman is coming on to me. I'll say no such thing.' He winked at Singh, who disliked the man more than he thought possible. 'So, she says why don't I come back to her place and have a shower. We all know what shower is code for, don't we, fellas?' Grant's grin made him look like a caveman. 'Anyway, that was the first time. Probably in the spring or summer.'

'Did you meet regularly?' Barrett's pen was poised above the notepad.

'About once a week for a few months. It weren't serious. Just animal sex. She couldn't get enough.'

'And where did you meet?' Singh asked.

'Usually on the common. Sometimes she'd be waitin' for me to run past and she'd grab me and we'd go off somewhere. She was a minx.'

'Such as?'

'Oh, sometimes the loos in the Fort pub.' *Classy*, Barrett thought to himself. 'Sometimes back at her place. But she liked doing it in public places most.' Grant's eyes sparkled with the memory, turning Singh and Barrett's stomachs.

'Who ended the relationship?' Barrett used the term loosely.

'Me.' Grant stiffened, and adjusted his position in the chair. 'She was gettin' clingy, so I called it off.'

'When?'

'Like I said, it went on for a few months, that was it. I didn't count.' Neither officer believed that for a moment.

'How did she take it?' Singh couldn't wait for the interview to be over, but was taking pleasure in being involved in the interrogation.

'She was upset, of course.' Singh chewed his lip in order to prevent a smile escaping. 'But she said her husband was suspicious and so it was probably for the best.'

'After the affair ended, did you see much of each other?'

'Nah, not at all.'

'So, it must have been a shock when you realised she was attending the same book club as your wife?'

'You can say that again!' Grant spat out the words.

'And when did this come to light?' Barrett knew what Marion Bolton had told him and was eager to find out if Grant's claim matched.

'One of the old girls in the book club was havin' a birthday party. I didn't want to go, but Shirl, my wife, said there'd be free booze so I went along. She was there. I couldn't believe my eyes. No matter how much free booze was on offer, that put an end to my fun when I realised Toni and Shirl were mates, well, you can imagine.' Grant looked genuinely concerned.

'Did you have any contact with Toni after that chance meeting?'

'Nope. I knew she didn't want it getting out – and neither did I. Besides, I knew she had a new husband so it was all in the past, where it belonged.'

'And you've never seen or spoken to Toni Jones since attending Mrs Bolton's birthday party?'

'No.' Grant's grey eyes were steady as he looked directly at Barrett, who sat back in his chair and cocked his head slightly to the side. Something was bothering him about what he'd heard, but he knew he needed to process the interview in his mind before he could settle on what that was.

'So, there is no way you fathered the child that Mrs Jones aborted a few weeks before her murder?'

'Not me, mate.' His gaze was steady and his eyes were cold.

'You're certain your wife had no knowledge of the affair?' Barrett asked.

'Trust me, mate, if Shirl had known, she'd have had my balls for earrings, and there is no way she'd have been friends with Toni. My wife is someone you don't want to mess with. She don't take no prisoners, if you know what I mean.' And Barrett believed he did.

Chapter 16

1.30pm 25 June

'That was the single worst thing I've ever had to do.' Elly sat in the passenger seat of the car, next to Palmer, staring out of the windscreen with a dazed expression.

'It doesn't get any easier.'

'Well that's good to know. Remind me why I wanted to become a police officer?' She reached into her bag, removed a bottle of water, and took a swig, leaving a lipstick mark, before offering it to Palmer, who declined.

'He was so young. Who's going to look after him now?'

'Technically, he's an adult.' Palmer frowned.

'Poor kid, and on his birthday of all days.' Elly took another sip of water. Outside, the sun was high in the cloudless sky and the car was sweltering in the heat.

'Back to the station,' Palmer said, turning on the engine. He cranked up the air conditioning so high that it was deafening and blew Elly's hair across her face.

'He's got his grandmother.' Elly tried to reassure herself that Dean would be OK. She didn't like the idea of the boy being alone in the depressing flat they had just visited. 'But he'll probably lose his home,' she said, wondering if that was such a bad thing.

'Place was a dump,' Palmer added.

'Yes, it was grotty.' Elly closed her eyes, enjoying the cold air that was blowing into her face. 'Do we think it could be suicide?' she asked suddenly.

'From the description of her injuries it would seem highly unlikely,' Palmer said, knowing full well why Elly had suggested it.

'I suppose we will know more when the pathologist has had more time with the body.' Elly fanned herself with her hand, watching the world go by.

'Pity the boy couldn't tell us any more about where his mother had been. It's an odd case, I'll say that much.'

'How many women were at the book club, who we've yet to interview?'

'I think four of them. No doubt the boss will want to talk to Shirley Grubb before too long. I wonder how his talk went with Grant.'

'We'll find out soon enough,' Elly said, as the car pulled into the Parkside police station car park.

*

'Mum's dead.' His hand shook as he held his mobile phone to his ear. 'Did you hear me, Nan? Mum's dead.'

'What you talking about, Dean?' He could hear her puffing on a cigarette, and was grateful she was sober enough to recognise who she was talking to. Peggy Cox had managed to come off the drugs ten years earlier, but had replaced her habit with a fondness for cheap vodka.

'The police just came. They found her this morning in the river.'

Dean wiped away the tears that ran down his face as he sat in the darkness of his bedroom. When the police left, he'd gone in there, closed the door and pulled his curtains closed.

'Nan?' Dean said, listening to his grandmother cough and splutter.

'Yes, give me a minute.' She continued to wheeze down the phone and Dean wondered if there might be another death in the family that day.

Janet and her mother had not been close, and they hardly saw one another, but since she had cleaned up her act – enough to stop the drugs at least – Peggy had tried in her own way to build a relationship with Dean. She would send him five pounds in a card every year for his birthday and she had visited them twice. Dean knew how much his mother had despised Peggy, but now she was dead, he didn't have anyone else to turn to.

'I need you, Nan.' The boy felt utterly alone.

'Have you got enough money for the train?' she asked, still puffing on her smoke.

'I can probably get it.' He had a friend he could ask, if the jar in the kitchen didn't have enough change in it.

'Good lad. You remember my address?'

'Not exactly,' he admitted, still sniffing, 'I'll get a pen.'

'Number twenty,' she said, the fag hanging out of her mouth, 'Hall Road. Nearest station is Dartford. You'll have to work out how to get 'ere from yours.'

'Thanks, Nan.' Dean felt a little relief.

'No bother, but I ain't got much in the fridge, so don't be expectin' a lot.' His relief evaporated.

'I won't.'

'Be a good boy and bring me some fags, and if you've got any drink lying around, no point leavin' it behind to go to waste.'

'Okay, Nan,' he said, as Peggy put down the phone without saying goodbye, let alone anything to comfort him.

He slipped his phone into the pocket of his black hoodie and looked around his bedroom. The place didn't feel the same; it was like it knew that his mum had gone. Grabbing a rucksack, he loaded his clothes into it and tried shoving his Xbox and some games on top, but they wouldn't fit. The only other place there might be a bag he could use was his mum's bedroom, so, with quivering legs, he closed his door behind him and went into the room next to his. Her single bed was still made and some dirty washing lay on the floor in the corner, next to the full laundry basket.

Rummaging through her wardrobe he found a small, brown fabric suitcase and pulled it out, dusting it off before getting out of the room as quickly as he could. It was as if he could feel her ghost in there.

He opened the tatty bag and loaded his console and games into it, as well as a pair of trainers, and a few tins of Stella he'd removed from the fridge. Unlike his nan, his mother hadn't been a big drinker.

Next, he checked the jar on top of the fridge, which was meant to be full of savings so they could go on holiday, but never had more than a few quid in it at a time; with the rent, the food and the bills, his mum never had much left out of her pay packet.

Unscrewing the slightly sticky lid, he emptied the change into the palm of his hand and pocketed it, not bothering to count it, but guessing there wasn't much more than ten pounds.

The police officers had asked for a picture of his mother so he didn't have the horrible job of having to go and identify her. He'd managed to find an old photo album and had given them one of Janet looking younger, happier and healthier.

Before leaving the flat, Dean decided to return to the photo album and have a flick through. He'd never paid much attention to family photos before, as it had always been just the two of them. He'd hated having to admit to the police that he'd never met his father and that his mother had always told him she didn't know where he was. He'd felt judged by them, even though they hadn't said anything. Dean had never had any time for the police. They'd given him enough grief for him not to trust them. So what, if he liked smoking pot? So what, if he took a car once without asking? As far as he was concerned, the police were nothing more than pigs.

At the front of the album, Dean spotted a picture of his mother holding him when he was a baby. He slipped it out and put it in his wallet. He wanted something to remind him of her.

Looking down at the two bags that contained the disappointing contents of his life, Dean punched and kicked the wall until his knuckles bled, before collecting his bags and leaving the flat for the last time.

*

'Amy, Christ! Come here,' Johnny bellowed from the kitchen. He was attempting to soothe the atmosphere by making his wife lunch. Black pudding, poached eggs and broad beans were on the menu.

Amy appeared in the doorway.

'The body they found today, it's Janet Cox.' Johnny looked ridiculous wearing his wife's floral apron. Amy couldn't help but smile at the sight of him, before his words began to sink in.

'What did you say?'

'Janet. The body in the river. The police are saying it was Janet.'

Amy walked across the kitchen like a zombie, before sitting down at the large, industrial, pine table.

Johnny, who was torn between comforting his wife and making sure the eggs weren't overcooked, decided to turn down the gas and attend to Amy.

'This is getting creepy now.' Amy looked at him with a horrified expression. 'Two from the book club? That can't be a coincidence.' She put her face into her hands and Johnny put his arm around her shoulders as they began to shake up and down.

'I didn't even like Janet,' Amy sobbed.

'I know.' Johnny was relieved his wife was allowing him to comfort her. There had been so much friction between them.

'What is going on? I don't feel safe. I want to get out of here, get away from Cambridge. It feels like the walls are closing in.'

'Whatever you want,' Johnny soothed. 'We could go and stay with my brother, up in Scotland. The break would do you the world of good.'

'Don't.' He felt her body tense and she shrugged him away. 'Just don't,' she repeated.

'So now I can't even console you when you're upset?' Johnny stood and walked away, angry, considering leaving the house. He turned and faced his wife. 'I can't go on like this, Amy. Either you forgive me or this marriage is over.'

She looked up at her husband and thought for a moment. 'Are you serious?' She stood and placed a hand on her belly, reminding him what was at stake.

'It was years ago. How long are you going to make me suffer for a mistake that is in the past? I wish I'd never told you.'

'You wish you'd never told me, or you wish you'd never slept with that slut?' Amy's glare burned with anger, and Johnny, who was at the end of his tether, sank to his knees and pleaded with his wife.

'Amy Martin, you are the love of my life. We are going to have a baby together, and we are going to get back to being happy, but you have to, you absolutely have to remember that I love you, and I will never, ever do anything like that again.'

Alarmed, and saddened at seeing her husband in such a desperate state, Amy too got down on her knees.

'Tell me her name.' She was calm and collected. 'Please. If you want this to stop, I need to know. It's torturing me. Tell me her name.'

Johnny's face fell and he closed his eyes. Amy watched as a single tear worked its way down his cheek. This was the moment they had both been leading to. She could feel it and she held her breath, feeling the blood pumping in her neck like a drum beating a countdown.

'OK, I'll tell you, but I need you to remember we had only been together for two months when it happened. Promise me you'll remember that?'

Amy nodded, still holding her breath.

'It was Alice, OK. It was Alice.'

Amy closed her eyes and slowly exhaled as the three words hit her like a punch to the chest. It was the name she had been dreading to hear, but the name she had expected all along. It was Johnny's turn to hold his breath.

Very slowly, Amy got to her feet, supporting her bump with a hand beneath it. She walked over to him and looked down. He remained on his knees, looking up at her, waiting for her to speak.

'OK.' She put her hand on his head and ruffled his dark hair. 'I forgive you.' He wrapped his arms around her calves and began to sob relieved tears of joy. 'Now,' she said coldly, 'get out.'

*

'I can't come to you because I don't drive, and my Terry is working.' Maggie was mildly excited at being contacted by the police.

'We are happy to drive over and speak to you at home, if that helps?' Palmer readied himself for another trip out.

'That works for me. What time shall I expect you?'

'Give us half an hour.' Palmer wanted a chance to grab a bite to eat before having to conduct another conversation.

'My kids are here. They won't bother us, but I thought I'd warn you. My Jamie will probably just stay in his room on his computer, and I'll tell Leigh to keep away.'

'Very well.' Palmer felt exhausted from speaking to her already. 'See you soon.'

'Bye.' Maggie hung up and rushed upstairs to speak to her children. 'Leigh, Jamie, get out here a minute.' Leigh opened her door, still in her pyjamas, having had a late night out with her college friends. 'Where's your brother?' Maggie stood with her hands on her hips.

'Probably has his headphones on,' Leigh yawned.

'Jamie!' Maggie knocked impatiently on his door. 'Jamie!' The teenager appeared, wearing a T-shirt and jogging bottoms, his hair sticking up in various directions.

'Right, you two, the police are coming to talk to me.' Maggie made it sound slightly more important than it was. 'I don't want you barging in and asking for breakfast or anything. If you're hungry get yourselves some food now, and, if you do see them, remember to be polite.'

'Why are they coming here, Mum?' Leigh showed interest, which pleased her mother. Jamie did not. 'They want to talk about,' Maggie moved a bit closer to her daughter and half whispered, 'the murders.'

'I'll be in my room,' Jamie said, leaving them to it and closing the door.

'Murders?' Leigh was confused by the plural use of the word.

'They found Janet Cox dead now an' all.'

'What?' Leigh, who was a bright girl, looked more concerned than thrilled by the revelation. 'When?'

'Today, in town.'

'Hasn't she got a son?' Leigh struggled to remember his name.

'Yes. Dean. A bit older than you.' It was the first time since hearing the news that Maggie had given any thought to the boy, and she felt a twinge of sadness.

'You alright, Mum?' Leigh asked.

'Yes, fine.' Maggie turned and headed downstairs. 'I'm just going to get that cake out of the freezer for the police. Nice to be able to offer them something.' The Richman family lived on Verulam Way, in Arbury – an area north of the city that had a reputation for being rough. The house was a 1960s semi that Terry and Maggie had bought twenty years ago, when they were newlyweds, with the intention of it being their family home. Maggie was especially house-proud and, luckily, Terry was willing to fully redecorate as often as his wife decided necessary, which was usually every two years.

Maggie bent down into the chest freezer, her bosom getting in the way, and fished out a large chocolate cake she'd made a few days before. Maggie always liked to be prepared: 'You never know who might drop in', was one of her many mottoes.

She defrosted the cake – in her professional standard microwave – and displayed it in pride of place on her dining room table. It was all she could do to stop herself from tucking in before they arrived; with twenty minutes to go before they were due, she busied herself with the washing-up that was piled in the sink.

Normally she would insist that one of her children did it, but she wanted them out of the way and needed something to do while she waited. Wrapping a kitten-patterned apron around her waist, she pulled on her pink Marigolds and got stuck in.

By the time she'd dried it all, put everything away in its place and made herself a cup of sweet tea, the doorbell was ringing. Quickly removing the apron, but still wearing a pair of fluffy slippers, she bounded towards the door and opened it with a warm smile.

Palmer and Barrett looked hot in their suits as they waited, the sun beating down on them. It was unusually warm for the time of year in England.

'Come in,' she welcomed them, her brown eyes smiling through her trendy, purple-rimmed glasses, 'go through.'

The officers did as they were told and made their way through the hall and into the dining room, which was off the kitchen. Palmer took particular notice of the jolly wallpaper, which was silver with large pink flowers.

'Tea, coffee?' she asked. 'Cake?'

To her disappointment both men declined.

'We'd like to talk to you about the night of the book club last week.' Barrett stood formally, with his hands behind his back.

'Oh, do sit down.' Maggie wanted them to relax, the formality was making her nervous. To her relief both men accepted the invitation. Through the net curtain, the sun poured into the room, casting a bright light over everything.

'What do you need to know?' Maggie also took a seat, crossing one leg over the other and making herself comfortable. Barrett noticed her slippers and smiled to himself.

'We'd like to know what happened at the meeting, if there is anything significant that you think we should know.'

'Well, there was a bit of a falling out, but I wasn't there for that.' Palmer noted that Maggie looked mildly disappointed. 'But I heard about it from Marion when I arrived. Toni stormed off just after I got there with Amy—'

'Is that Amy Martin you are referring too?' Barrett interrupted.

'Yes. She's a real good friend of mine. We often make our way to whoever's house it is together. Anyway, Kim left, and Toni, and then Pauline. It wasn't much of a book club that night. Not sure we did any talking about the book we'd been reading,' she snorted.

'What was your relationship like with Toni Jones?' Palmer asked.

'We were civil.' Maggie looked slightly uncomfortable. 'She wasn't my favourite person, but I would never have wished any harm on her.'

It seemed to the detectives that this was a running theme with a number of the people they had questioned.

'She could be quite funny, sometimes, when she wasn't being a cow.'

Barrett could tell she was about to launch into a long monologue, so he quickly cut in, 'And what about Janet Cox? When was the last time you saw her alive?'

Maggie was only just getting used to the idea that Janet was dead too, having only heard an hour ago.

'Well, I wasn't that fond of her either.' Maggie adjusted her glasses, aware that the policemen might think she wasn't a very forgiving person. 'She was manipulative. Passive aggressive too. I wouldn't have trusted her as far as I could throw her.' Palmer had a mental image of Maggie lifting Janet over her head and tossing her into the water. It was ludicrous, but it remained in his mind nevertheless.

'Is there any reason in particular that you came to that conclusion?' Barrett asked, curiously.

'You know what, I can't put my finger on it. I've thought about it. I suppose it was to do with the way she behaved. She was hot one moment and cold the next. A bit like Toni, I suppose, but with Toni you always felt like maybe she had a reason for behaving how she did. Janet, well she jumped to conclusions about people and could be really quite mean.'

'And when was the last time you saw her?' Barrett repeated his question.

'Oh, yes, it was on Saturday. We all met at Amy's house after we heard what had happened to Toni.'

'Whose idea was that?' Palmer asked.

'I think Marion was the one who rang round,' Maggie said, trying to remember the sequence of events. 'Pretty sure it was Marion, but Amy called me.'

'And what did you talk about when you all met?' The detectives were unaware that the gathering had taken place, and took a special interest in Maggie's answer.

'We just met to sort of ... console each other I suppose.'

'But you say you weren't particularly fond of Toni?' Palmer's eyes narrowed.

'I wasn't, but she was one of us in a way, and we'd only seen her a couple of days before.' Maggie felt the pressure of the question weigh heavily on her.

'I see.' Barrett waited for her to continue.

'Well, we met, and I brought some cakes,' she pointed to the untouched chocolate sponge sitting in the middle of the table, 'and we were just going to talk about it.'

'Did everyone who attended the book club go to Amy's house that day?'

'Mostly, but not Pauline. She wasn't there. Kim was late, as usual,' Maggie rolled her eyes, 'and everyone else came on time I think. There was,' she uncrossed her legs and put her hands on her knees, 'a bit of an argument.'

'Between who?' Barrett raised his eyebrows.

'It actually started between Shirley and Amy.' Maggie was cautious not to land her friend in any trouble and chose her words carefully. 'They used to get on really well, Shirl and Amy, but things had got a bit sour between them recently. Shirl just suddenly seemed to turn on Amy. None of us really knew why, but I think it was jealousy. Shirl envies the life that Amy is carving out for herself. That's what I think anyway.' Maggie folded her arms across her chest. 'It is sad, really. Can't be nice always wanting what someone else has. Must make her unhappy.'

'Was Janet Cox involved in this argument at all?'

'Yeah. Those two are, sorry, *were*, as thick as thieves. Janet was like Shirl's skinny shadow,' Maggie chuckled. 'Like Laurel and Hardy.' She smiled again, before realising she was speaking ill of the dead. 'Well, anyway, they were really good mates, Shirl and

Janet, so when Amy and Shirl argued, Janet got involved and said her piece. She had a venomous tongue that one.'

'I see.' Barrett jotted something down in his notepad, but to Maggie's frustration, and despite her best efforts to look, she couldn't see what.

'Anyway, it had been headed that way for months. There was a lot of tension in the group. I don't suppose it will survive now that …' She didn't finish her sentence.

'Can you think of any reason why someone would want to harm either Janet or Toni?' Palmer knew it was unlikely that Maggie would have the answers, but he watched as she cocked her head to one side, ran her hand through her silvery purple hair, and thought about it.

'There was a lot of bad feeling among members of the book club. No point pretending there wasn't, but nothing that was anything more than a bit of bitching and a few strained friendships.' She shrugged, but then appeared to remember something. 'Is it true you arrested Pauline?' Maggie's eyes twinkled.

'Mrs Robinson,' Palmer cleared his throat, 'was helping us with our enquiries for a time.'

'So you did! Well, well, butter-wouldn't-melt Pauline, who'd have thought it.' She seemed to be enjoying herself.

'We are no longer pursuing that line of investigation,' Palmer said, putting her straight, not wanting any unnecessary gossip to be spread.

'Fair enough. Do you think the deaths are linked? I mean, is someone targeting the book club? Should I be worried?' Maggie suddenly appeared much less sure of herself.

'We are investigating every possibility but, as far as we are concerned, there is no cause for alarm. Of course, we would advise everyone to be extra vigilant at the moment until the culprit—'

'Or culprits,' Barrett interjected.

'Or culprits,' Palmer repeated, 'have been caught.'

Maggie had hoped to gain more information than she had, but was not really surprised that the police were keeping their cards so close to their chests. There was no doubt the case would be jeopardised if they told everyone what they were thinking. Still, she felt a pang of disappointment.

'Are you sure you won't have some cake? My chocolate sponge and buttercream icing is famous in these parts.'

Not wanting to offend her, Palmer asked if they might take a piece back to the station to share out among the team. Thrilled that her cake was finally being welcomed, Maggie insisted on boxing the entire thing for them to take back with them. Barrett stood on the doorstep and thanked her for her time, while Palmer left carrying a large white box.

Chapter 17

4.15pm 26 June

Barrett sat behind his desk with a face like thunder. The investigation seemed to be stalling and he was impatiently waiting for the results of the post-mortem. It seemed unlikely that Janet Cox had gone into the water where she was found, and as soon as that was confirmed, which he was certain it would be, he could get on with searching for the scene of the murder. The longer that took, the more likely it was that any forensic evidence would be lost or damaged, and the thought did not please Barrett, or his team.

Due to the suspicious nature of the death, they had to wait for a pathologist from the Home Office to do the post-mortem. Barrett knew there were rules and processes, and most of the time he agreed with them, but once in a while, when an investigation was hindered by bureaucracy, he wondered why such practices existed. Surely, catching a killer was more important than following protocol?

But Barrett had been in the force long enough to know that there was no point dwelling on it. There were other things he could be getting on with while he waited, and he had – he'd interviewed everyone except Amy Martin and Shirley Grubb, and he would be the first to admit that he'd had talked to enough women to last him a lifetime. He found them to be complicated creatures, and he struggled to decipher important information from what was, simply, waffle.

When Palmer appeared looking flustered, Barrett knew it must be because he'd received a call regarding the post-mortem results.

'Right.' Palmer, slightly breathless, was holding the notes he'd jotted down while listening to the pathologist. 'She did not go into the water where we found her.'

'I knew it,' Barrett said, matter of fact.

'The pathologist explained that the diatoms in her blood did not match those in the water where she was found.' Barrett stared blankly at Palmer. 'Oh, yes, that was my reaction too,' Palmer chuckled. 'Diatoms are tiny animal life forms that live in the waterways. The same way a soil sample will differ from one field to another, so will the diatoms in the water. The pathologist is going to head out and take a number of samples from further up the river, to see if they can conclude where the body went in. The other thing the discovery of the diatoms means, is that she was alive when she went into the water. Had she been dead, there would have been no blood circulation, therefore, no diatoms could have ended up in her blood.' Barrett nodded, following every word as closely as he could. 'Having said that, the pathologist confirmed there was blunt trauma to the skull, and the victim would have died as a result of a brain haemorrhage had she not drowned first. In other words, she stood no chance.'

'How quickly will the pathologist be able to collect and analyse the water samples?'

'She said that she and the SOCOs are going to do that this evening. They should have the results by tomorrow. She also said that there is no evidence on the body that Toni Jones was raped, and that, because so much time has passed since the alleged rape, it would have been unlikely that there would be any sign anyway.'

'Okay.' Barrett got up and did his typical thing of pacing back and forth. 'We have two more people to interview. I'd like to speak to Amy Martin first. Let's leave Mrs Grubb until last.' Palmer knew Barrett's reason for doing this was because he didn't relish the prospect of potentially having to break it to the woman that her husband was a scoundrel.

'Yes, sir. She lives on Mawson Road, off Mill Road. It's a five- or ten-minute walk.'

'Good,' Barrett said, looking out of the window. 'I like a late afternoon stroll in the sun.'

The walk from Parkside police station to 102 Mawson Road was not quite as pleasant as Barrett had hoped. Mill Road was bustling with students out enjoying the sun, and people sitting on the street, outside cafés, drinking coffee and having a bite to eat. It was also busy with bikes, and the cyclists had no concern about riding on the pavements, despite the number of pedestrians they endangered and had to swerve around. By the time the detectives arrived, Barrett was once again in a grump.

When the red front door opened, both men were slightly surprised to see a pregnant woman in her thirties. She looked tired, and did not offer more than a brief smile to the strangers.

'DCI Barrett.' He held up his badge. 'Are you Mrs Amy Martin?'

'I was,' she replied wistfully. The men didn't grasp what she meant. 'I mean, yes,' she said, with an apologetic look.

'We understand that you are a member of the book club that both Janet Cox and Toni Jones were members of, is that right?'

'It is.' With her left hand, she held the edge of the door, her right was rested on her bump. Palmer noticed that her protruding belly button could be seen through her thin white top.

'May we come in?'

'Sure. I wasn't expecting anyone so the place isn't very tidy.' She tucked a loose piece of dark hair behind her ear and Barrett noticed a tan mark where a wedding ring should have been.

'We aren't here to judge the state of your home,' Palmer said kindly, as he followed her into the living room. On either side of the Victorian fireplace there were shelves stuffed with books. The room had a mix of vintage and modern furniture and Palmer noticed how different it was to the homes of the other book club members they had visited. It reminded him more of the kind of home you found in the trendy parts of London. Shabby chic was the description that sprung to his mind.

Amy curled up in a faded velvet armchair while both officers sat on the brown leather sofa.

'It's awful what's happened to those women. Makes me shudder every time I think about it.' Amy chewed her fingernail.

'How well did you know them?' Barrett noticed a painting on the wall that he liked.

'Outside of the book club we didn't spend much time together. Apart from the books, I didn't have a lot in common with either Janet or Toni.' *Ain't that the truth*, Palmer thought to himself. 'I got on well with Toni at first, but never really Janet. It didn't seem to matter though. We weren't all there to be best friends. We just got together to talk about what we liked reading and share our opinions.' Amy looked over at a vase of irises that were dying. They were a present from Johnny on his return from London. She'd been meaning to throw them out.

Both Barrett and Palmer noticed the sad look on her face and wondered what the cause was.

'So, you wouldn't say you got on very well with Janet Cox?'

'No, I wouldn't.' Her blue eyes looked at him and Barrett felt the blood rush to his checks.

'Why is that?'

'She was a snake. Rude and untrustworthy. Is that reason enough?' Palmer put his hand over his mouth to conceal a smile.

'Where were you on the night she was murdered?' Barrett fired back, determined not to be intimidated by the pregnant woman who showed no fear.

'I won't sit here and pretend I'll miss her, just because you are policemen. I've had enough of manipulative liars, thanks very much.'

'Is everything alright?' Palmer leant forward, clocking the tears in the corners of her eyes.

'Not really. I kicked my husband out and now I am facing being a single mother. To top it off, when all I really want to do is lie in bed and cry my heart out, I have to sit here and talk to you about a woman I couldn't give a damn about.'

Barrett wasn't sure if he admired or disliked her frankness. One thing he was certain about, was that there was no way this woman was a killer. She may not have liked Janet Cox, or Toni Jones, but she had more important issues going on in her life than bumping off two women.

'Look, let's put it this way: all that glitters isn't gold, and Toni was a chav.'

'Not exactly how I'd describe her.' Barrett's brow furrowed.

'No, not in the typical sense, but she behaved like one. She asked for trouble, she had a chip on her shoulder, thought she was bigger and better than she was, and her idea of banter was making other people feel small. I call that chavvy.'

'And Janet Cox?' Palmer asked, amused by her analysis.

'Oh, Janet was just a skank. One of the most insincere people I've ever met. I really didn't like being in her company.'

'Don't hold back, will you?' Barrett was shocked.

'Why should I? I've nothing to hide. Would you rather I pretended everything was rosy and forced a smile? As I'm sure you already know,' she said, wiping away a tear, 'I argued with Janet, and Shirley for that matter, the last time I saw her alive. But thinking someone is a skank isn't reason enough to murder them now, is it?' Neither Palmer nor Barrett could argue with that, or had any intention of doing so.

Disarmed by her fragile yet fierce state, the officers thanked her for her time and excused themselves, noting the boxes in the hallway containing men's clothes and some records.

Palmer felt sorry for her as he pulled the door closed, leaving her all alone with her anger and sorrow.

'She's a handful,' Barrett puffed.

'Never mess with a pregnant woman, sir.' Palmer winked.

'So it would seem.' He half laughed, still trying to process what exactly had just taken place inside Number 102.

'Next?' Palmer asked, already knowing the answer.

'Shirley Grubb.' They both knew the time had come, but neither of them were looking forward to what lay ahead.

*

Amy poured herself a glass of homemade lemonade and sat in the kitchen looking at the boxes in the hall. Her heart hurt and she wondered if she'd ever feel happy again. Why did Johnny have to sleep with Alice? She knew it had happened years ago, before they got married, but that wasn't the point. He'd cheated on her and lied about it, made so much worse by the fact it was with his ex-girlfriend. Amy knew how broken-hearted he had been when his relationship with Alice had ended. Alice had taken a job in Paris and called off the relationship, saying she didn't do long distance. Johnny was fragile when he met Amy. He'd told her how much he'd suffered when Alice had moved away, and Amy could see the damage she'd left behind.

After Johnny and Amy had met, and started their relationship, Alice briefly returned to London. Johnny's version of events was that Alice had appeared at his flat one night, telling him how she still loved him and that she regretted the break-up. He and Amy had only been together for two months and he'd given in to temptation. But Johnny swore blind that the next morning he had asked her to leave and never come back. According to Johnny, he'd told her that he was in love with Amy and that he'd moved on; Alice had taken the news well and they said their goodbyes. He'd never seen her again after that.

Sitting at the kitchen table, aware of how quiet and lonely the house seemed, Amy wondered why he'd chosen now to confess. It was in the past, she didn't need to know. But from the moment he'd admitted it, it was all Amy could think about. She felt betrayed and she couldn't help but question the last three years of their life together. What else might he not be telling her? If he could do it once, Amy was fearful he could do it again, despite all his apologies and promises that there would never be a repeat of that night with Alice, or anyone else.

Now Amy was pregnant and felt more alone than she'd ever experienced. Removing her mobile phone from her denim shorts pocket, she scrolled through her list of contacts until she found Johnny's number. Her finger hovered over his name, wanting to stroke it. She was tired of being angry and tired of feeling hurt. She loved her husband and wanted things to be the way they had been before he'd confessed about his one-night stand.

For the first time since she had found out about his indiscretion, Amy wondered if perhaps she had overreacted. Did she really want to throw away her marriage because of one mistake that had happened years earlier? Did she want to raise the child growing inside of her alone? She thought about Toni and about the damage that her affair had done to her marriage. This was not the same. This was very different.

As she looked down at her husband's name, Amy decided not to call him just yet. She still felt raw and needed more time before she could make a decision about their future. She returned the phone to her pocket and drained a glass of cool lemonade as the doorbell rang.

England was in the grip of a mini heatwave and she groaned at having to get up again. Her lower back was tender and she felt sweaty.

Opening the door, Amy was surprised to see a delivery man holding a huge bunch of irises. She signed for the bouquet and stepped indoors, closing the door behind her, knowing who had sent them.

'I will not give up. I love you,' the note read, and Amy smiled to herself as she returned to the kitchen to arrange the flowers in a vase. In that moment, Amy knew exactly what she was going to do.

*

Maggie stood in her kitchen fanning herself. The kitchen window was open but it made no difference to the heat. She couldn't stop thinking about Janet's son, Dean. It was true that she hadn't been close to Janet, but as a mother she worried about the boy. She knew Janet had no family in the area and wondered what would become of him.

Rather than show up at Janet's house unannounced, and interfere, she decided it would be best to call Kim to discuss her concerns. Normally she'd be on the phone to Amy, but she knew Amy had enough to deal with already.

She leant against the kitchen worktop, holding the phone to her ear and hoping that Kim would pick up.

'Hello, chick,' Kim said, in a voice that almost purred.

'You alright?' Maggie asked.

'Yeah, you know, sitting in the garden with the kids. We got the paddling pool out and I'm seriously thinking about getting in myself,' she chuckled.

'Sounds like a good idea. If only my kids weren't too old for paddling pools.'

'I'd swap your kids for mine right now.' Kim laughed again.

'No, you wouldn't.'

'No, you're right, it's just in this heat they are finding it difficult to sleep. The house is so hot so they're all pretty grouchy.'

'I know the feeling!' Maggie said.

'Anyway, enough about the kids. How are you?'

'Oh, I'm fine thanks. Not brilliant, but okay.' Maggie paused, not sure exactly what the purpose of her call had been. 'I guess you've heard the news about Janet?'

'Oh yeah. What is going on? Two of us in less than a week. I don't like this one little bit.'

'I know what you mean. I'm keeping my front door locked when I'm in the house, you know, just in case.' Maggie couldn't help but feel a bit stupid by her admission.

'Yeah, I've told Pete he has to work from home at the moment. I don't want to be left on my own with the kids when there's some nutter out there.'

'You think it's a random nutter?' Maggie asked.

'I don't know. Why, what do you think?'

'I think it's someone we know, for sure.' The words made Maggie feel queasy.

'Really? Who?' It seemed that thought hadn't occurred to Kim.

'I dunno. Wouldn't like to say either, but it's not a coincidence, is it?'

'No, I guess not.'

'Anyways, I didn't call you so I could play Miss Marple.' Maggie wanted to move the conversation on. 'I was calling because I've been thinking about Dean.'

'Yeah. Poor kid.' Maggie could hear that Kim was smoking.

'Shouldn't we do something? Go and see him? Check if he's okay?'

'I suppose we could.' Kim didn't sound as enthusiastic as Maggie had hoped.

'He's got no family around here, has he? We could just take him some shopping and make sure he's taking care of himself.' Maggie had always been a kind person.

'It's a nice idea, but none of us really know him, do we?' Kim had a point.

'But Shirley does, doesn't she?' Maggie planted the seed.

'Yeah, Shirl knows him.'

'Well, maybe you could call her and suggest she drops by to check on him? I'm not really speaking to her, after what happened at Amy's house.'

'I'm not sure I should get involved.' Kim was doing her best to avoid any responsibility. She knew Shirley would be upset by the death of her friend and wasn't looking forward to having to talk to her about it.

'We could all chip in for a hamper, or something. She could just drop it round.'

'Mags, he's nineteen. He won't want a hamper. More likely booze and fags!' Kim had a point.

'Alright, not a hamper, but something. Maybe we could do a collection and give him some money to help tide him over?'

'Not a bad idea.' Kim said, watching the twins playfully wrestling in the water and seriously contemplating joining them when the conversation was over.

'I'll call round everyone and you speak to Shirl, yeah?' Maggie encouraged.

'Yeah, leave it with me.'

'Okay. Good.' Maggie was satisfied that she was doing the right thing. 'We should do something.'

'I'll call Shirl now.' Kim slipped off her flip-flops and went and stood in the cold water. It felt so good. 'Speak in a bit,' she said, sitting down, not minding that her blue cotton dress was getting soaking wet. The twins looked at her in amusement before deciding what she really needed, was to be splashed. A lot.

Chapter 18

12.30pm 27 June

Barrett put down the phone and marched out of his office into the incident room.

'Right, I need your attention,' he said, clapping his hands together and silencing his team. 'I've heard back from the pathologist. As suspected, Janet's body did not go into the water in the city centre. After taking various water samples, they have concluded that the body went into the water somewhere in the Stourbridge Common area.'

A mutter went around the room.

'From injuries to the victim's skull, they have removed splinters of wood. It seems she was beaten with something wooden before being tossed, or falling, into the water. We know that Toni Jones died as a result of similar injuries. We also know these women knew each other, and both attended the same book club. It appears that the murder of Toni Jones was planned. The geranium petals seem to give weight to this theory. However, Janet's murder was different and her injuries, although they would have proven to be fatal, were not as frenzied as the injuries of the previous victim. Therefore, I suggest we treat this as a crime of opportunity. The SOCOs are currently searching for the weapon that was used on Janet. The pathologist has confirmed that the splinters are sycamore wood. There are a number of sycamore trees growing on Stourbridge Common. For now, we will work on the assumption that the killing was not premeditated.'

'Do we know what was used to kill Toni Jones?' Elly asked.

'From the severity of the injuries, the pathologist has confirmed that the murder weapon was most likely made of metal. She has suggested something similar to a large Maglite torch.' Barrett looked down at his notes. 'There is one woman left to interview, but in the meantime, I want you all to dig into the lives of both dead women, and work out what else, if anything, links them.'

Everyone nodded and went back to work, while Palmer approached Barrett with a theory he'd been considering.

'Sir, what if Janet Cox knew more about Toni's murder than she was letting on? I'd say that was a pretty good motive for our killer, and it would explain a few things.'

'I'd come to the same conclusion myself, Joe,' Barrett agreed.

'I think this gives us even more reason to interview Shirley Grubb. If Janet knew something, perhaps she confided in her friend.'

'Yes. But first I want to organise a reconstruction. See if we can jog the memory of anyone who might have been in the area that night. Then, let's bring her in. It's about time we had a chat with Mrs Grubb.'

*

Having finished her morning shift, Shirley made her way to Milton Road to pay a visit to Dean. To her surprise, she discovered a few bunches of flowers leaning up against the front of the bookmakers as a tribute to Janet. Her heart sank as she was reminded of what she'd lost. She'd considered calling Dean first, to let him know she was coming, but she didn't think it best to speak to him on the phone. In reality, she wanted to see him to pass on her condolences and check that he was coping on his own.

After nipping down the side alley that led to the flat's entrance, Shirley stood outside and knocked on the door. She then rang the doorbell, and called out his name, but Dean didn't answer. She panicked. She needed to know where he was. Perhaps he was with a friend? Janet would never have forgiven her if she turned away and did nothing, so Shirley took her phone out of her bag and tried Dean's number, struggling to remember why she'd ever been given it in the first place.

His phone rang four times before it was answered.

'Dean. It's Shirley.'

'Hi.' He sounded miserable.

'Where are you? I'm outside the flat.'

'I'm stayin' with my nan.'

'In Dartford?' Shirley was surprised, knowing what a volatile relationship Janet had had with her mother.

'Yeah. Didn't wanna be in the flat.' Shirley could understand that.

'I'm glad you're safe. How long are you staying there for?' Although she'd heard plenty of bad things about Peggy from Janet, Shirley felt relieved to learn that the lad wasn't alone.

'Dunno. Haven't thought about it yet. Is there any news on Mum?' He sounded choked.

'Sorry, Dean. I haven't heard anything.' Shirley went and stood next to her car and leant against the hot metal.

'What about the funeral?'

'I don't know. Have you spoken to the police?'

'They know where I am and stuff.' He sniffed.

'You could call them. I'm sure they'd answer your questions.'

'I dunno what to do.' He sounded lost. 'I've not had to arrange a funeral before. Don't even know how to pay for it. Mum didn't exactly have loads of savings.' Shirley knew this much was true.

'I can help. I'm sure your nan will too.' This, she wasn't so sure about. 'I think you did the right thing, leaving Cambridge. It wouldn't do you any good being stuck in that flat.'

'It's a dump. Always has been. Glad to be out of there to be honest. Nan's isn't exactly Buckingham Palace, but it's better than that shithole and she lets me do what I want.' To Shirley's way of thinking, that probably wasn't a wise decision on Peggy's part, but she said nothing.

'Do you need anything? I've still got the spare key. I could get some things sent over to you, if you want?' She looked down at the bunch of keys in her hand and rubbed the one belonging to the flat between her fingers.

'I took some stuff but I left my black trainers behind. Send them.' As usual, his manners failed.

'OK, I'll do that. Is there anything else you want?'

'Nah, nothing.'

'Text me your nan's address, I'll put them in the post later today.'

'Will do.'

'And, Dean, I'm really sorry about your mum.'

'Yeah, well.' He clearly didn't feel comfortable with her sympathy.

'Take care of yourself, alright? If, or when you come back, let me know. I'll make sure to do a shop so you don't starve. I know what you teenagers are like.'

'I'll text ya,' he said, and hung up.

Since her conversation with Kim the previous day, Shirley had managed to collect over £200 from the surviving women in the book club. Even Amy had chipped in a decent amount, which surprised Shirley, knowing how Amy had felt about Janet.

As she entered the flat, she decided she'd fold the money and put it into one of the trainers she was planning to post, but the thought evaporated as soon as she was hit by the stench of rotting rubbish. The bins hadn't been emptied and the room was buzzing with flies that had taken advantage of the fact.

Holding her nose, she went into the kitchen and removed the putrid sack of rubbish from the bin, gagging as she did so, and placed it just outside the front door. For some reason, the flat seemed smaller than she remembered. On the occasions when it had been Janet's turn to host the book club, she'd always suggested that they met at a café, or a pub, using the excuse that her place was too small. Shirley, having known it was a spacious flat, had always suspected that Janet was slightly embarrassed by it, but standing there she felt bad for having ever thought that. Shirley should have known better. Janet was never really embarrassed by anything, and certainly not her home.

Shirley felt uncomfortable being in the flat alone, as if she was encroaching on Janet's privacy. The place was a mess and Shirley knew Janet would not have wanted her to see it looking like that, even if it was evident it was normally in a similar state. Looking around at the sparse furniture and all Janet's belongings, Shirley wondered what would become of them.

Deciding not to dwell on it, she went in search of Dean's trainers in his bedroom. His cupboard was open, as were his drawers, and they had been emptied. The room smelt stale, the kind of smell that only existed in the bedrooms of teenage boys. Shirley had had enough of bad smells at work and hadn't bargained for them in the flat as well.

The duvet was pulled back in a pile at the end of the bed, and posters of cars, and women with their breasts out, covered the walls. Shirley didn't quite know where to look, and she rushed around the room, feeling again like she was somewhere she shouldn't be. Finally, after checking under the bed, she discovered the black trainers Dean had referred to, and bundled them into an empty Sports Direct bag that lay discarded on the floor. She finished just as her phone began to ring. Not recognising the number, she answered, while standing in the doorway of Janet's bedroom.

'Mrs Grubb, my name is DCI Barrett. I'm investigating the murders of Toni Jones and Janet Cox. I understand you knew both victims?'

'Yes.' Shirley had not been expecting the police to call her.

'We'd like to talk to you about the last time you saw both victims alive. Would you come to the station as soon as possible please, to give a statement?'

'Can't I do it over the phone?' Shirley asked, clearly irritated by the request.

'It would be better if you came to the station, Mrs Grubb,' Barrett said in a serious tone. 'It won't take long.'

'Well I'm kind of busy now. Can I come later? I've got to go to my daughter's sports day.'

'Are you available at five?' Shirley looked at her watch. It was 1pm.

'Yes, I can be there then, but I don't know what you expect me to say. I can't help you.'

'We just have a few questions, Mrs Grubb. Two women are dead. This is a serious matter.'

'Yes. OK. I'll be there at five.' She made no attempt to hide her annoyance.

'Thank you. We'll see you then. Please ask for me at the desk when you arrive.'

'Will do.' Shirley hung up the phone in a bad mood. Her day had just got worse; she'd been dreading sports day as it was. The sports field had no shade on it, so she'd have to sit in the direct heat while her little darling competed. Now, to top it off, she would have to spend time talking to the police, when all she really wanted to do was go home and sit in front of the electric fan.

Slamming the door behind her, she stomped down the stairs, and away from the flat, without a thought of Janet.

'She wasn't very eager to come and talk to us,' Barrett said to Palmer.

'I wonder why.'

'I think the phone call interrupted something. And anyway, you should remember, Joe, not everyone is on our side. Some people have a problem with the police.'

Palmer nodded, recalling times in the past when he'd had to deal with such people.

'Still, I'd have thought she'd be keen to find out what happened to her friends.'

'She probably is, but it doesn't mean she is going to relish the idea of talking to us.' Barrett twiddled his thumbs as he sat at his desk.

'Are you going to mention the affair between her husband and Toni?'

'I've not decided yet. I'll make the decision once I've met her and looked her in the eye. Now that Janet Cox has also been killed, it seems unlikely that the affair is relevant.'

'What about the abortion? We still don't know who fathered the child.'

'No, we don't, but we do know that Toni Jones had been having an affair during her marriage to Mike. The abortion just goes to prove she still couldn't keep her knickers on.' Barrett frowned, frustrated by the lack of knowledge they were still contending with.

'There's no sign of her having been in contact with another man, from either her phone or her computer,' Palmer added.

'Well she was clearly having an affair. There must be a trail somewhere. We just haven't found it yet.'

'But, sir, even if that's true, what does that have to do with Janet's murder?'

'I don't know yet, I just have this feeling that it comes back to that abortion.'

Palmer had witnessed his boss's hunches on a number of occasions and, if one thing was certain, more often than not Barrett was right, although he wasn't so sure this would turn out to be one of those occasions.

'Is it possible Mrs Jones had another phone? Something separate so she could contact her lover?'

'We've checked and there is only one mobile phone in her name.'

'God damn it.' Barrett slammed his fists down on his desk. 'Every avenue seems to lead to a dead end. When will there be a break in this bloody case? I've got the superintendent breathing down my neck.'

'We'll get there, sir,' Palmer tried to soothe his boss, knowing they were all feeling the pressure, 'it's just a matter of time.'

'Let's just hope another woman doesn't show up dead before we do "get there",' Barrett said, dismissing Palmer with a wave of his hand.

'Perhaps the interview with Shirley Grubb will give us more information,' Palmer said, standing in the doorway, preparing to close the door behind him. 'I mean, if she knew her husband had had an affair, that would be a motive right there.'

'I disagree,' Barrett said woefully. 'Why kill a woman your husband used to sleep with? Why wait all this time? No, I don't think Shirley Grubb is our killer, but she may prove helpful yet.'

'Yes, sir,' Palmer said, sighing as he left the room. He was used to having Barrett shut down his ideas, but he still hadn't got used to it. One thing he did know was that his theory about a serial killer being on the loose wasn't too far wrong. Now two women were dead, and Barrett's words about another body showing up were ringing in his ears.

Chapter 19

3pm 27 June

Amy was relieved when she received an email from Marion suggesting that the book club be cancelled until further notice. She'd decided that she no longer wished to attend, but hadn't got around to letting them all know and this saved her that hassle. From what she could gather, a number of the women were disappointed it was going to be cancelled. Reading the email thread, she could see that Barbara and Pauline in particular had voiced their sadness. Amy knew how much it meant, especially to Barbara, and hoped that Marion would still agree to meet her so she had some company other than her cats.

Amy had been on the phone to Maggie recently, who suggested putting together a collection for Janet's son. Despite the fact she had little time for Janet, Amy was not a bad person, and she agreed to donate a reasonable amount of money, stating there was more where it had come from, if needed.

As she sat in her living room with the shutters fastened, she closed her eyes and enjoyed the cool air being circulated by the large fan she had set up in the corner. She was not enjoying being pregnant in the heat one bit, even less so since waking up to discover a strange note had been pushed under her door.

On a strip of white printer paper, which had been folded in two, there were only two typed words: YOU'RE NEXT.

She'd stood in her slip reading it over and over, before deciding that she would call Johnny and ask him to come home. When she'd told him about the note he'd advised her to call the police.

'Do you know if either Toni or Janet received a threat like that?' The concern in his voice was tangible.

'I don't know. There's been nothing about it in the press,' she admitted. 'It's probably a wind-up; a hoax or something.' But even as she said it she didn't feel so sure.

'I'm coming back now. Lock the doors and keep your phone with you. It's a long drive but I'll be back this afternoon at some point.' Not knowing what else to do, Johnny had driven up to the Lake District to stay with his brother, giving Amy the space she'd said she needed. He now wished he'd gone to stay with a friend in London instead. Whether the note was a hoax or not, the fact was that two women had been murdered already and he didn't want Amy to take any chances. 'I'll come as quickly as I can,' he told her, already packing his bag. 'I love you.'

There was an uncomfortable pause as Amy considered her response.

'I love you, too,' she said before hanging up, and she had meant it.

Amy kept glancing at the clock on the wall. She'd spoken to Johnny at 9am and was expecting him home at any moment. Looking forward to his arrival, and having decided she wanted to try to forgive him and make a go of their marriage, she'd put all of his belongings, which she'd boxed, back where they belonged. Seeing his shirts hanging in the wardrobe once more had made her feel good. Things were as they should be.

What she didn't know was, at that moment, Johnny was lying in hospital with a punctured lung and a broken arm, in a critical condition, having been in a car accident on the motorway as he was speeding home to her.

He had been racing back to Cambridge, driving faster than usual, in order to reach Amy. His concern, having heard about the note, was palpable. There was a killer on the loose and two of his wife's acquaintances were dead. Was she next? The fear encouraged him to press harder on the acceleration pedal and, when he was on the M1, not far from Nottingham, one of the front tyres had burst, sending the car into a spin. It had only taken a few seconds for his red Audi to smash into a blue Peugeot, before crashing into the barrier that separated the carriageways. The bonnet was crumpled and Johnny was unconscious in the driver's seat; blood poured down his face, his arm at a peculiar angle, his chest pressed against the steering wheel.

*

'Sir, we've had a call from the Nottinghamshire constabulary. There has been a road traffic incident on the M1. Three cars were involved and two people have been taken to hospital with serious injuries. It appears that one of those involved was Johnathan Martin, the husband of Amy Martin. He is in a critical condition and is currently in surgery. We've been asked to inform his wife,' Elly said.

'We were with her a little while ago.' Palmer shook his head with disbelief.

'You'd better go and speak to her.' Barrett waved Elly on her way. 'She may well need to be driven up to Nottingham. Which hospital is he in?'

'Nottingham University Hospital,' Elly said, checking her notes.

'Just what we don't need,' Barrett growled. 'Be as quick as you can.'

'Yes, sir,' Elly said and nodded, before disappearing out of the room, a serious expression on her face. She didn't relish the task of delivering bad news to anyone, but surely, it couldn't be worse than having to tell a teenager that his only parent was dead?

'There is something else,' Palmer cut in before Barrett could bark any further orders. 'A mobile phone has been discovered in the river near where Janet Cox went into the water. We believe the phone might belong to the victim. It's with forensics now.'

'Good.' Barrett looked satisfied for the first time that day. 'Shirley Grubb is expected here in one hour.' He checked his wristwatch. 'I want to go over the statement from her husband before she arrives.'

'I'm going to get a coffee, do you want one?' Palmer asked, knowing the answer already.

'Yes. Black, no sugar.' They had been working together for a few years, but still Barrett told him, every single time, how he took his coffee. 'I'll be in my office.'

Palmer nodded and made his way towards the coffee machine, wishing instead that he was heading to the pub for an ice-cold beer.

*

Elly stood on the front porch waiting for Amy Martin to open the door. She was regretting wearing a black top and leggings as she felt the beads of sweat run down her neck.

Amy opened the door smiling, clearly expecting Elly to be someone else.

'Mrs Martin?' Elly spoke softly.

'Yes.' Amy looked at her suspiciously.

'I'm DS Elly Hale. Is it possible to come in?'

'I've spoken to your lot already today.' Amy appeared mildly irritated.

'We need to speak to you about your husband.'

'Why?' Her eyes narrowed with suspicion.

'It would be much better if you'd let us come in.'

'Very well,' Amy said, letting Elly and her companion, yet to introduce himself, past.

Once the three of them were in the kitchen, Amy softened and offered them some lemonade. Both officers declined.

'I'm sorry to tell you that it appears your husband has been in an accident.' Elly couldn't help but fixate her gaze on the pregnant bulge of Amy's stomach. 'He was involved in a road traffic accident and is in a critical condition in Nottingham University Hospital.'

Horror instantly plastered Amy's face.

'A car crash?'

'Yes,' Elly confirmed.

'When did this happen?' Amy's head began to swim and she felt a wave of sickness.

'This afternoon. I've been instructed to drive you to the hospital.'

'Is he going to be alright?' Her voice was hoarse.

'He is in surgery.' Elly was not prepared to make any false promises. 'Is there someone you'd like to call?'

'No.' Amy looked around the kitchen, as if she was in a foreign place.

'We should probably leave now, Mrs Martin.'

'Yes, yes.' Amy scrambled around searching for her keys, mobile phone and handbag.

Elly and DS Singh, who had remained silent since arriving, stood and waited patiently by the kitchen table while she collected her belongings. Something on the table caught Singh's eye. A white piece of A4 paper lay next to a vase of irises. On it were the words: YOU'RE NEXT. Removing a pair of latex gloves from his pocket, he picked it up and showed it to Elly.

'Can you tell us what this is?' Singh asked Amy when she reappeared in the kitchen clutching her handbag.

'It came through my door this morning.' Her voice was trembling.

'Do you know who sent it?' Elly asked.

'No idea.' It was the last thing on Amy's mind at that moment.

'Didn't you think to report it?'

'No. I'm sure it's just a hoax.' Amy was desperate to leave the house. She wanted to be with Johnny.

'Given the current investigation, Mrs Martin, this could be vital evidence.' Singh's tone was unforgiving.

'I don't care about that right now. Please, I just want to see my husband,' Amy pleaded.

'I need to take this to the station.' Singh turned to Elly. 'You drive her. Did it come in an envelope?' Singh asked, turning to Amy again.

'No. It was just folded and shoved through my letterbox.' Amy was getting frantic and Elly decided it was time for them to leave.

'I'll drive Mrs Martin up to Nottingham,' Elly agreed.

'I'll call the boss,' Singh said, getting his phone out of his pocket.

'Let's go.' Elly smiled kindly at Amy and guided her out of the house, towards the car, just as Singh managed to contact Barrett.

'Sir, I have something that I think you'll want to see,' he said, holding the note up so the daylight was behind it. 'I found a threatening letter lying on Mrs Martin's kitchen table. She says it was delivered this morning, but I'm not so sure …'

*

By the time Shirley arrived at Parkside she was beyond hot and bothered. After sports day had ended, she'd had the mother of all rows with Kayla. She had wanted to go shopping in town with her mother's credit card and was firmly told no, at which she had exploded into an ugly teenage rage.

Once at home, Kayla had stormed up the stairs and slammed her door so hard that the entire house shook. Shirley discovered that Grant had not mowed the lawn as he had promised, and she found him sitting in the living room, in his pants, watching a World Cup football game.

Not wanting her husband to know that she'd been called in to speak to the police, Shirley made an excuse that the book club was meeting and left her hopeless husband and foul-tempered daughter at home to feed themselves. She was not in the mood for cooking, even if it would only have involved removing some nuggets and chips from the freezer and putting them in the oven.

The traffic was slow and the air conditioning in her car had packed up, so by the time she turned up for the interview she was not feeling much like talking.

Barrett and Palmer ushered Shirley into the interview room and sat opposite the red-cheeked, sweaty woman, who had a face like thunder.

'Thank you for taking the time to come and talk to us.' Palmer had decided to play good cop.

'It's fine,' she said, although the officers could see from the expression on her face that it clearly wasn't.

'We'd like to know a bit about your relationships with both victims.' Barrett watched the beads of sweat collect on her temples – a result of the interview room having a lot in common with a sauna.

'I've known Janet for a good few years.' Shirley realised she was talking about Janet as if she was still alive, but continued anyway. 'She's a good friend. Always had my back, you know?'

'Outside of the book club, did you spend much time together?'

'Oh yeah, quite a bit. She was a bit lonely. I think she found it tough raising Dean on her own.'

'Do you know anything about the young man's father?' Barrett did not like the fact that so much mystery surrounded him.

'A bit. Janet told me it was a one-night stand. She was young and when she told him about the baby he said he wanted nothing to do with it.'

'I see.' Palmer despised those kind of men.

'As far as I know, he moved away not long after Janet fell pregnant and she's never seen him since. She never mentioned him much. It was a long time ago.' Shirley wiped the sweat off her face with the back of her chubby hand.

'Did she ever tell you his name?'

'Not sure she did. As I said, she didn't mention it much.'

'And what about your relationship with Toni Jones? Were the two of you close?'

'She was a good friend.' Shirley smiled fondly. 'I liked her. She was feisty.'

'Can you tell us anything about the night of the book club?'

'Probably nothing more than you've already heard. Women gossip, Chief Inspector, in case you didn't know.' Her eyes twinkled with amusement and Barrett could sense she was thawing.

'I'd like to hear it from you, if it's all the same.'

'Well, there was a bit of a barney. Some things were said. I can't remember exactly what, but it all got a bit awkward. Kim left, Toni left. In the end, most of us left without discussing the book we'd been reading. I think it's the weather, you know. Everyone feels sensitive in this heat.' Shirley blew her fringe out of the way as if to emphasise the point.

'How long have you known Toni Jones?' Palmer cocked his head to one side slightly, trying to read the woman opposite him.

'A while now. Not as long as Janet. We met through an online book club. Maybe, five years ago. Maybe longer. We chatted online and got to know one another. She was funny online. Said what she thought, didn't hold back. Bit of a diva, if you know what I mean?' Barrett nodded. 'Well, when we realised we lived in the same place, we agreed to meet up. Used to have coffee sometimes, that sort of thing.'

Palmer had heard all of this before and was growing increasingly frustrated by the lack of progress.

'When she suggested that we all get together for a physical book club, I thought it was a great idea. So many people hide behind their keyboards, don't they? All those bloody internet warriors.' She sighed. 'Anyway, so that was how it came about.'

'Can you think of any reason why anyone would want to hurt Mrs Jones?'

'You mean kill her?' Shirley asked steadily. 'No. No idea.'

'And Janet Cox?' Palmer asked.

'Janet was a good person.' Shirley looked sad. 'I can't imagine anyone wanting to hurt her.'

'Do you know if Mrs Jones had any secrets?' Barrett asked slowly.

'What kind of secrets?'

'Any kind. We understand that her first marriage ended because of an affair she had. Can you shed any light on this?'

'I didn't know her then.' Shirley shrugged. 'I met her just when she was getting together with Gerald.'

Barrett and Palmer shared a look.

'Did you know she'd had an affair?'

'Not at the time. It was only after she died I heard a rumour. But I don't see what that's got to do with anything.'

'We are just trying to build a picture of the victim, and your relationship with her.'

'Well, I'm telling you, she was my friend.'

'I understand that most of the members of the book club are married?'

'Yes,' Shirley said, wondering where the questioning was leading.

'Did you spend much time together as couples?' Barrett was nonchalant, but Shirley could see there was something more behind his question.

'Hardly ever. Grant isn't exactly the type. We don't do stuffy dinner parties or ask people over much. I've got my friends and he's got his.'

'So, you never spent time all together?' Palmer asked again.

'Once in a while I suppose we did.'

'Any particular occasions that spring to mind?'

'The only time I can ever remember Grant meeting everyone, was at a party for Marion's birthday.'

It crossed his mind for a moment that all the women in the book club were in it together. No matter where Barrett turned he was given the same answers. He was sick and tired of dodging the issue and decided to go for the kill.

'Are you happily married, Mrs Grubb?' Barrett leant in, fixing her with his gaze.

'Why'd you ask that?' Shirley frowned.

'We are just trying to build a picture of everyone who is a member of the book club.'

'I've been with Grant for years. He's not perfect, what man is?' She winked at Palmer, who thought it highly inappropriate. 'But we're happy enough,' she concluded.

'And you have one daughter together, is that right?'

'Yes. Kayla. She's thirteen going on nineteen.' A brief moment of anger crossed her face.

'And I understand that Kayla is adopted.' Barrett looked at his paperwork.

'Yes.' Shirley stiffened. 'What has my daughter got to do with any of this?'

'I'm simply checking my facts.' Barrett could see that he'd touched a nerve.

'The facts,' Shirley sneered, 'are this. Two of my friends have been killed, and as far as I can tell, the police have done very little except interrogate a group of women who are all members of a book club. You should be ashamed of yourselves. My dad always said the police couldn't be relied on. He was right.'

'I'm sorry you feel that way, Mrs Grubb.' Barrett took pleasure in putting emphasis on her surname.

'I'm not intimidated by you lot,' she said, smiling.

'Our intention is not to intimidate you. We are simply investigating all possible avenues. A double murder is as serious as it gets.'

'I agree, so why don't you stop wasting my time and get out there and catch the man responsible?'

Not yet ready for her to leave, Barrett put a clear plastic bag on the table. Inside, for her to see, was the note that had been left for Amy.

'This was left at the address of a fellow book club attendee. Do you recognise it?'

Shirley leant over to read it through the bag. 'No,' she said, sliding it back across the table towards Barrett.

'Have you received anything like this in the last few weeks?'

'No, but even if I had, I wouldn't be coming to you lot about it,' she snorted.

'I think that's enough for now.' Barrett got up, his chair squeaking across the floor. 'We'll be in touch if we need anything else. Palmer, show her out.' Barrett was not inclined to say goodbye to Shirley and he left the room without even a glance in her direction.

Chapter 20

6pm 27 June

Maggie was beside herself when she picked up the phone to Marion. Her hand trembled as she gripped her mobile, willing Marion to answer sooner rather than later.

'Hello?'

'Marion, it's Maggie.'

'Ah, hello, pet. Everything alright?' Marion immediately recognised the panic in Maggie's voice.

'Not really. Johnny, Amy's husband. He's in hospital. He's been in a car crash. It doesn't sound good.'

'Good grief. Is Amy alright? And the baby?'

'They weren't in the car.' She paused, grateful that Amy and her baby were safe. 'Look, I hate to do this, but I need a favour. I've tried Kim, but she can't help.' Maggie spoke quickly, not drawing breath. 'She's got the twins and Dylan and can't get away. I mean, I would ask Terry, but he's working late.'

'How can I help?'

'I need a lift.'

'No problem. It ain't far to Addenbrookes.'

'No, Marion, that's the thing. He's in hospital in Nottingham. That's where he was when he had the accident.'

'What was he doing there?'

'He was on his way back to Cambridge.' Maggie resisted explaining any more. 'And I just got the call from Amy. She's in an awful state. The police are driving her up there but she's all alone. He's gone into surgery.'

'Don't say another word.' Marion could always be relied on in a crisis. 'Let me get Arthur's dinner on the table and then I'll come and pick you up, pet. Give me half an hour.'

'Thank you.' Maggie thought she might cry. 'Thank you so much. I didn't know who else to call.'

'You did the right thing. That poor girl shouldn't be on her own. She'll need her friends around her.'

'That's what I thought.'

'All this stress can't be doing her any good.' Marion remembered back to the days when she was pregnant. 'You did the right thing. Make yourself a cuppa and wait for me. I'll beep when I'm outside.'

'Great. Thanks, Marion. See you soon.' Maggie hung up and dashed around the house getting a few things together that she thought might be useful. She put some crisps and fruit in a bag, along with a book she thought Amy would enjoy, as well as a jumper in case it was cold in the hospital.

Trying to ignore her memories of sitting in hospital waiting for news about her father-in-law, she made sure that she left a note for Terry and the kids, explaining where she'd gone and what had happened, before taking herself outside to sit on the wall and wait for Marion.

As the sun began its slow descent from the deep blue sky, Maggie sat contemplating all the bad things that had happened since the last book club meeting, and she couldn't help wondering to herself if everyone who had attended was now somehow cursed. How many more tragedies could they withstand? She wasn't sure of the answer, but one thing was certain: Johnny had to survive. The alternative was unthinkable.

*

As Amy sat in the back of the car, staring out at the fields that were rushing by, she had a similar thought to Maggie. It was almost unbelievable how many things had happened during that week. She couldn't believe she'd sent Johnny away. The accident was her fault. If he'd been at home … that thought alone made her feel ill. How could she have been so stubborn? With what had happened to Toni and Janet, why hadn't she found it within her to forgive him earlier? She cursed herself and promised, from that moment, she would never take her life or her husband for granted again.

When they passed the sign for Loughborough, Amy knew they weren't too far from Nottingham and she clamped her clammy hands together in anticipation. She would make it up to Johnny. He would get better, they would have their baby, and they would be happy again. The alternative was too awful to consider.

Willing the car to go faster, Amy could feel Elly watching her in the rear-view mirror. The detective was most likely younger than Amy, and she found herself wondering if she had a family or a husband.

'Not too long now,' Elly said, as if reading her mind. 'I appreciate this is a difficult time for you, but can I ask again why you didn't report the threat you received?'

Amy had forgotten all about the note. 'I had other things on my mind.'

Elly nodded without believing her. 'I'm sorry, but if it was me, and two women I knew had been murdered, I'd want to tell the police if something like that came through my door.'

'I'm sure you would, but I didn't.' Amy stared coldly at Elly, who turned her attention back to the road ahead and went quiet, knowing it wasn't the best time to question Amy, but struggling to contain her feeling that there was something more to the situation.

'Can we change the subject please? My husband is lying in hospital. Some stupid note is not my top priority right now.'

'Of course.' Elly couldn't stop herself from adding, 'but I think it's only fair to warn you that the DCI will want to talk to you again.'

*

'I can't believe it,' Marion said, putting the car into reverse and pulling away from the curb. 'Whatever next?'

'I know,' Maggie agreed, fastening her seat belt. 'It is unbelievable. One thing after another at the moment.'

'Do you know what happened?'

'Not really. It was a crash. He's got a punctured lung.'

'That's not good.' Marion wondered if Johnny would survive.

'No,' Maggie replied, as she tried not to think about what Amy would do if her husband didn't pull through.

'It's a two-hour drive. We'll be there by nine.'

We'll be lucky if we make it there in one piece, Maggie thought to herself, as Marion took the corner at breakneck speed, nearly hitting a cyclist and hooting the horn, much to Maggie's embarrassment.

Wanting to distract herself from the terrifying journey she was facing, Maggie changed the subject.

'Have you heard any more about the investigation?' She gripped the door handle until her knuckles were nearly white.

'Not really. Just what's in the news. I hear they are planning a reconstruction of the night Janet was killed. Morbid, if you ask me.'

'I suppose they think it might jog someone's memory. It is hard to believe that two women were killed in a busy city and no one saw anything.'

'Well, that's a good point.' Marion accelerated so she didn't miss the green light on the crossroads.

'Doesn't it scare you?' Maggie asked, not sure whether she was referring to the speed at which Marion was driving, or the threat that a killer had them in their sights.

'You've been reading too many horror books,' Marion chuckled, as the car joined the motorway.

'I'm more worried for my kids. What if someone breaks into my house when they're at home?'

'You're forgetting something, pet – motive.'

'There is never a good reason to take a human life,' Maggie said.

'Well that's true, but you're not thinking like a killer. You're thinking like a rational person. Anyone who kills isn't the same as you or me.'

'You've got a point,' Maggie agreed, wondering what it was that could push someone over the edge enough to justify murder. 'I couldn't kill anyone.'

'Well, neither could I, but if someone hurt my family I might be persuaded otherwise ...'

Holding her breath while Marion overtook a very large lorry at lightning speed, Maggie wondered if that was true. If someone hurt her kids, she'd certainly want revenge, but murder? She supposed she would never know exactly how she'd react.

Not wanting to contemplate anything happening to her kids, Maggie returned to thinking about Amy and Johnny. It wasn't a scenario she enjoyed conjuring up.

The rest of the journey was spent in relative silence, both women trapped inside their own heads, contemplating the action that had taken place over the last week.

Marion, who had hoped the book club would survive, had now resigned herself to the fact it was truly over. The relationships within the group were fractured beyond repair and it had stopped being fun. She worried about what would become of Barbara, and decided that she would arrange to meet her once a week, as they always had done, and the two of them could visit gardens together since they shared a passion for flowers. They could still discuss books, if they wanted, but she doubted it would ever be the focus of their conversations again. The realisation came as a mixture of sadness and relief.

'It's sad that the book club is over.'

'Yes, it is. But it stopped being fun some time ago.'

'I suppose it did.' Marion thought back to the last few meetings. 'What do you think happened?'

'I dunno. It just changed, didn't it? The atmosphere wasn't right.'

Marion considered this and wondered when things had changed. Was it one thing that had happened, or a sequence of events? She wasn't sure.

'I hope we will still see each other.'

'I'm sure we will,' Maggie said buoyantly. 'I'll always have cake waiting.'

'You know I'm a glutton for your flapjacks.'

'I'll make some especially for you. To say thanks for driving me to the hospital and all.'

'I'm very fond of Amy. You needn't thank me.' Marion took the car off the motorway and followed the signs for the hospital. 'We'll be there soon. I'll drop you out the front and go and find somewhere to park. No point in us messing about and wasting time. That girl needs us.'

Maggie smiled at Marion calling Amy a girl, as she was far from it, but appreciated the intention.

'Let's hope Johnny is going to be OK.' For a moment, Maggie had an awful fear that she'd turn up at the hospital to discover he'd died. That wasn't something she'd bargained for when leaving Cambridge.

Whatever the situation, she had come to support her friend, and that was exactly what she was going to do. If the worst had happened, Amy would need Maggie more than ever.

Chapter 21

9am 28 June

Amy had been sitting in the relatives' room in the intensive care unit since arriving at the hospital; she was now sandwiched between Marion and Maggie, while DS Elly Hale sat on the other side of the room flicking through a battered magazine.

The operation to fix Johnny's broken arm and deal with his punctured lung had taken much longer than the surgeon had first anticipated, and the wait had been long and anxious. Amy burst into tears when they were informed that he had made it out of the operating theatre alive, but the doctor had warned that he was far from being out of the woods yet.

Thankfully, Maggie and Marion had arrived in time to hear the news and support Amy. It had been a long, uncomfortable night for them all.

Amy was horrified to learn that other people had been injured in the crash, and that a woman in her twenties had also been hospitalised. It would seem that Johnny had been speeding, which is what had caused the crash. Amy felt more guilty than she had ever thought possible. If only … the words spiralled around her head.

Amy had not slept a wink, unlike her three companions, who at different points had managed to drift off for various lengths of time.

During the night she had spoken to local police officers who'd attended the scene of the crash. They informed her that CCTV footage confirmed that Johnny had been driving faster than the legal speed limit, but that the crash was caused by a burst tyre, which meant the car had spun out of control. The officer explained that no charges would be brought against anyone, which made Amy feel slightly better, but not much.

All she wanted was to be able to see him. After his surgery she'd been allowed to see him as they wheeled him up to ICU, but the nurses had encouraged her to return to the relatives room until he was conscious, which was where she'd been stuck for nearly twelve hours. Throughout the night she'd visited the nurses' station to ask when they thought he might regain consciousness, but none of them were willing or able to answer. It was a case of being patient, they explained, which was something that didn't come naturally to Amy.

'I know you're worried, pet, but you really should eat something. You need to keep your energy up, for you and the baby.' Marion placed her hand on Amy's tense shoulder.

'I've got food.' Maggie fumbled in her rucksack for the crisps she'd packed.

'No. I can't. I'd just be sick.' Amy got up and began pacing backwards and forwards; the sound of her flip-flops slapping the bottom of her feet echoed around the room.

'He'd want you to look after yourself,' Maggie said, removing a packet of ready salted from her bag.

'He'd want not to be stuck in the hospital, struggling to breathe, strapped up to machines.' Amy sniffed back tears. That silenced them all. No one could argue with that.

*

Shirley arrived promptly at work. Her boss had said she could take a few days off to grieve for her friends, but the Grubbs needed the money so Shirley had no choice but to keep on working.

Hinton Grange had got gradually hotter with every day that the heatwave continued. It made the smell of the place more pungent and, therefore, the work more gruelling. Incontinent elderly people and hot weather were not a great mix. The place stank of urine and low-cost ready meals. Most of the residents were tired and bad tempered as a result of the heat and Shirley, who normally enjoyed the sunshine, found herself wishing it was midwinter.

As she stripped the beds and bundled the stinking sheets into the washing trolley, she tried her best to think about nicer things, but the death of her friend sat heavily on her mind. She missed Janet. Janet was the best friend she'd had and she wondered if she would ever have such a good friend again. Shirley had never really cared for most of the women in the book club; she got on well enough with Kim, but felt she was very much in Amy's camp, and she certainly no longer had any desire to be friends with Amy.

Once upon a time she and Amy had got on, but in recent months their relationship had soured. Amy didn't approve of Shirley's sudden closeness to Toni because she saw it for what it was. That had left Shirley feeling uneasy and unable to relax in Amy's company, which had cast a shadow over the whole group. What Shirley couldn't understand, was why Amy cared if the friendship was hollow; Amy had shown recently that she had little time for Toni, so why did it matter to her? Shirley would never understand Amy's position: Amy didn't like Toni and she refused to lie, and pretend that she did, or use her.

Underneath it all, Shirley resented the fact that Amy had the conviction to be honest. Shirley's grasp of loyalty had always been loose.

By lunchtime a dark patch of sweat had appeared on her uniform, below her bust, and her bra was rubbing. Her hair had taken on a life of its own and resembled a mane.

As she sat in the staffroom eating her lunch, her mobile phone vibrated in her pocket informing her she'd received a message. Struggling to slide the phone out of her tight pocket, she huffed and puffed before finally being able to read it.

Babe, you around today? I need to see you. We need to talk xxx

The message was sent from Kim. Shirley looked at the message, blinking. She was not expecting to hear from Kim, as they didn't often have much contact. There was also something about the tone of the message that made her feel uneasy.

Sure sweets. Working now. Finish at 2, can come after. All OK? Xxx

Shirley hit send and a minute or two later her phone beeped again with a response.

See you then xxx

Shirley, like most people, knew that Kim loved a drama, but she was fascinated to find out what it was that Kim needed to talk to her about. It seemed convoluted, but it certainly piqued Shirley's interest. She spent the next hour trying to guess the reason for the conversation ahead.

*

All the windows in the incident room were open and two fans had been set up, but the heat remained oppressive.

Palmer sat at his desk waiting for a forensic report. The SOCOs were convinced they'd discovered the heavy stick that was used to crack Janet Cox's skull. That, twinned with them having recovered her mobile phone, meant the investigating team were hopeful there might be a development with the case. In the meantime, they had to sit tight and wait. It was frustrating, being stuck inside in the heat, unable to do much. DS Singh had been tasked with tracking down Janet's iCloud account, but these things were never as quick or as simple as most civilians presumed.

To make matters worse, they had been receiving drunken phone calls from Peggy Cox, wanting to know when they would be releasing her daughter's body for burial. A number of officers had taken it in turns to try and explain that the pathologist needed more time before releasing the body, but the aging, drunk woman didn't seem able to retain the information she was being told.

Gerald, too, had shown up at the station, wanting to know if the investigation was making strides. Julie, the Family Liaison Officer assigned to his case, was deeply apologetic to the DCI and his team, but it was clear that she had little control over the grieving husband. Every member of the team could feel the pressure building and the temperature outside was doing nothing to abate the situation.

Barrett, who was looking out over the green space of Parker's Piece opposite the station, was struggling to fill in the gaps. He treated every case like a jigsaw and he felt that some of the pieces were missing in this one. He hoped that before long the tide would change and the police would find themselves on top of the case, because, as much as he wanted to get his superiors off his back, he wanted to get justice for the victims' families.

Although it seemed likely that the murders were linked, the police had to explore the idea that it could be a coincidence. It was their job to look at things from every angle, no matter how unlikely certain scenarios might seem. It was time-consuming, but their responsibility to follow the ABC of policing: assume nothing, believe no one, challenge everything. The problem was that the team had applied this mantra to the investigation, but they were still struggling to come up with a solid motive, let alone a suspect.

Barrett watched as a group of schoolkids kicked a ball about on the green during their lunch break. He wondered how anyone could contemplate playing football in that heat and never failed to be impressed by the resilience of young people. That thought led him to consider Dean Cox: what would happen to him? He was pleased that the boy was with his grandmother, or at least he had been until she'd started calling the station and ranting like a lunatic, but Barrett knew as well as anyone that family relationships could be complicated. It was one of the reasons he avoided his own.

'Sir, sir!' A shout came from the other side of the incident room and Barrett spun around to see DS Singh hopping up and down next to his desk. 'I've managed to access the iCloud account of Janet Cox. You need to come and see this.'

*

Amy, who had been sitting by Johnny's bedside, had called the nurse when she noticed he was turning blue and the machines he was hooked up to had started beeping. She was quickly ushered into the relatives' room while the doctor rushed to examine him.

Amy had been waiting five minutes for some news when a troubled looking nurse appeared in the doorway of the relatives' room.

'Amy, I'm afraid I've got some bad news.' Her face was pale and her hands were clenched together. 'There has been a complication. I'm afraid your husband's lung has collapsed; we are doing everything we can and are preparing him for surgery.'

'What does it mean?' Her heart pumped furiously in her chest and she could feel her pulse throbbing in her temples.

'The doctors will do everything they can. He's in safe hands. The aim of the surgery is to remove the damaged tissue that has caused the pneumothorax.'

Amy stared blankly.

'Collapsed lung,' the nurse corrected herself.

'Are there risks with the surgery?'

'Every surgery carries a minor risk,' she answered steadily.

'Can I see him before he goes in?' Amy was shaking and Maggie had come to her side and slipped her arm around her friend's shoulder. Marion sat, frozen to the spot, shocked and terrified in equal measures.

'The anaesthetist is on his way. You'll have a minute or two but please, keep it brief.'

Amy nodded and rushed out of the room, leaving Maggie and Marion wondering what to do with themselves while their friend was possibly saying goodbye to her husband for the last time.

Chapter 22

2pm 28 June

Shirley was in the staff room collecting her bag and preparing to sign out. Her colleague, Ruby, was enjoying a cup of tea and some peace and quiet during her fifteen-minute break.

'Anything nice planned for this afternoon?' Ruby asked, dipping a digestive biscuit into a milky cup of tea.

'I'm going to see my friend, Kim.' Shirley was not in the mood for making small talk with Ruby, but since Ruby was her senior she decided she'd better play nice.

'Oh, have a lovely time. I'm on till six.' She sighed, looking at the clock on the wall.

'Hopefully you won't get any trouble. They're all too wiped out from the heat to kick up much fuss at the moment.'

'I know how they feel,' Ruby chuckled, as half of her soggy biscuit fell into her tea. 'Damn,' she said, trying to scoop it out with her fingers.

'See you tomorrow.' Shirley smiled, pleased to be leaving work.

'See you then.' Ruby was sucking her biscuit-covered fingers as Shirley left.

She'd wondered if she would ever have another friend as good as Janet, and Kim's text gave her hope that she might. It was clear that Kim wanted to confide in her about something, and she'd chosen Shirley over everyone else, which made her feel special.

On her way to Kim's house on the Lynfield Lane, in Chesterton, close to Stourbridge Common, Shirley stopped off at a petrol station and picked up a bottle of wine. She knew how keen Kim was to drink, and that day she fancied a glass or two herself. It had been a stressful week.

As she pulled up outside Kim's house, Shirley felt a tingle of excitement. Her day was about to get a lot better. She'd always enjoyed Kim's company, even if she was a bit gobby and had a tendency to drink too much. Blowing off some steam with a bottle of wine and amusing company was just what she needed.

Still in her uniform, she smoothed her fringe before knocking on the door. She was grateful for the small amount of shade the porch offered, and, as the door opened, she held up the bottle with a beaming grin.

Kim looked summery in her faded denim skirt and pastel yellow T-shirt.

'I brought supplies!' Shirley stepped forward and gave her friend a hug, noticing that the embrace was not exactly reciprocated with warmth.

'I'll get some glasses. Why don't you go into the garden?'

Shirley followed Kim through the house, disappointed – and unnerved – by the stiff welcome she'd received.

'The kids not here?' she asked, looking around.

'No. The twins are still at school and Dylan is at nursery for the afternoon. Bliss.' Kim smiled as she reached for two large wine glasses that were on a shelf. 'It's too bloody hot to be indoors. Come on.' Kim led the way into the garden and the women sat down at a table that was shaded with a large parasol.

'How've you been, sweets?' Shirley asked, unscrewing the cap on the warm bottle of white wine.

'Yeah, not too bad. Difficult to do anything in this heat.' Kim held out a glass.

'It's been a mental few days,' Shirley said, pouring.

'Yes.' Kim looked as if she was about to say something, but changed her mind.

'Have you got any plans for the summer?'

'Pete wants us to get a villa in Spain. I said we should invite his mum to come so she can help look after the kids,' Kim chuckled.

'Good idea.'

'What about you? Going anywhere?'

'Maybe a few nights in Butlin's, if I can get the time off work, and if we can afford it,' Shirley replied.

'That'll be nice.'

The pair sat silently, sipping their wine. Kim didn't think of herself as a snob, but she could tell if wine was cheap, and the bottle Shirley had provided certainly was. She put down her glass, not wanting to drink any more vinegar.

'Awful what happened to Janet,' she said, looking at Shirley and waiting for her reaction.

'Yeah, I know. I can't believe it.'

'I know you were close.'

'She was a good mate.' Shirley nodded, looking down at the reflection in her glass. 'I'll miss her.'

'And Toni,' Kim paused, 'it's just unbelievable. I can't get my head round it.'

Shirley nodded, and sipped her wine.

'The police don't seem to have a clue.' Kim pulled her sunglasses down from her head and over her eyes.

'Useless.' Shirley curled her lip in disgust before draining her glass. 'Have you spoken to the others much?'

'You mean the book club girls? A bit. Have you heard about Johnny, Amy's husband?'

'No?' Shirley put her glass on the table and raised her eyebrows.

'He was in a car crash yesterday. He's in hospital.'

'How awful,' Shirley said, but Kim thought she saw her disguising a smug grin.

'He might not make it.' Kim watched her closely from behind her sunglasses, but Shirley's face had returned to normal and gave nothing away. Had she seen her smile? Suddenly Kim wasn't so sure.

'So,' Shirley said, changing the subject, 'you wanted to talk to me about something. Is everything alright?'

This was the moment Kim had been building up to but, now it had arrived, she felt herself freeze and her throat tightened. Could she really go through with it?

'What is it?' Shirley could see there was something very wrong.

'I dunno how to say this, chick,' Kim lifted the sunglasses off her face, 'but there is a rumour going around.'

'A rumour?'

'Yes,' Kim swallowed, it was now or never, 'about Grant and Toni.'

'What kind of rumour?' Shirley's eyes narrowed.

'That they had been having an affair.' Kim held her breath, waiting for Shirley's reaction.

'Well, it's not true.' Shirley dismissed it as if it had been the wrong order at a restaurant. 'Complete rubbish.'

'I'm not saying it isn't, but,' Kim chewed her lip, 'there's a bit more to it than that.'

Shirley's eyes burned into Kim's. 'What else?'

'My neighbour,' Kim pointed over the garden fence, 'well, her daughter is at school with Kayla. It seems Kayla's been saying that her dad was sleeping with Toni and he killed her.'

Shirley remained expressionless.

'She's been telling people at school that if they mess with her, then her dad will come for them.'

Shirley laughed, much to Kim's surprise. 'That's mental. Completely mental.'

'Well,' Kim felt herself blush, 'that's what I said, but I thought you should know.'

'Kayla always did have an overactive imagination.' Shirley poured herself another glass of wine and Kim thought she saw her hand tremor.

'I didn't know how to tell you,' Kim continued, 'but I thought you should know. Something like that could do a lot of damage. Especially while there is a murder investigation going on.'

'It's bollocks. All of it. Bollocks.' Shirley watched Kim, realising there was more to come.

'The other thing that she's been saying, is that her dad got Toni pregnant.'

*

After seeing the recording that was saved to Janet Cox's iCloud account, Barrett, Palmer, and a number of other officers ran out of the building and got in their cars; they now knew who was responsible for the murders, and it was time to arrest them.

*

'He's made it out of surgery.' The nurse who had earlier delivered bad news, was smiling as she gave Amy the update. 'He is stable. We are going to keep him heavily sedated for the moment, but you can go and see him, if you like.'

Amy's shoulders dropped and she smiled over at Marion and Maggie. The relief on her face was a joy to see.

'Thank you,' Amy said, as she hugged the nurse.

'We'll need to monitor him carefully but the operation was a success.' The nurse, who had been on a long shift, looked tired but equally relieved.

'Go and see him, pet,' Marion encouraged. 'Maggie and I will go and get some food in the concourse. Do you want us to get you anything?'

Amy turned as she was leaving the room. 'Yes, please. I want a double cheeseburger with everything on it.' Her smile informed her friends that she was back to her good old self and everything would be okay.

*

'That's not possible.' Shirley was quick to dismiss the idea.

'I'm not saying it's true, but it's what Kayla has been telling people.' Kim felt awful for having to break the news, but thought it better that her friend knew so she could do something about it.

'That girl.' Shirley's eyes burnt with rage. 'How dare she?'

'It's probably just for attention.' Kim leant over and rested her hand on her friend's arm. 'I thought you'd rather hear it from me, in case the police come knocking.'

'Why would the police come?' Shirley's voice growled.

'Oh,' Kim felt flustered, 'I don't know. They might want to talk to Grant. Or you.'

'Me? Why would they want to talk to me?'

This was the moment Kim had been dreading most.

'Because Kayla says that you knew and you did nothing about it.' Shirley sat quite still for a moment, examining Kim's face.

'Is that right?' she said, smiling.

'I just wanted you to know what was being said. You know what rumours are like. They spread and can get out of control.' Kim felt uncomfortable all of a sudden. Something about Shirley's reaction wasn't right.

'And have you repeated this rumour to anyone?'

'No, of course not!' Kim was indignant, despite the fact she'd discussed it with her husband and a few friends.

'Well,' Shirley said, standing up, 'it would be a real mistake if you had.'

*

The police car came screeching into the car park of Hinton Grange care home. Barrett leapt out of the car and rushed into reception.

'Where's Shirley Grubb?' he shouted at the surprised woman sitting behind the desk.

'She left.' The woman pointed to the door. 'Her shift was over.'

'Where was she going, Ruby?' Barrett read the woman's name badge as he flashed his ID and Palmer joined him at the desk.

'She told me she was going to see a friend.' Ruby looked confused and frightened, like many of the residents of Hinton Grange.

'Who? Which friend? I need to know.'

'Oh, erm ...' Ruby struggled to recall the conversation they'd had in the staff room, which had taken place an hour ago. 'Kim, I think. I think she said her name was Kim.'

Palmer and Barrett shared a grave look.

'Thank you,' Palmer said, and both men turned, heading back towards the car park.

*

'What's the matter, Shirl?' Kim asked. 'I mean, don't shoot the messenger. I never said it was true, or that I believed it. I thought I was doing you a favour.' Shirley stood, towering over Kim, her silhouette blocking out the bright sunlight.

'You're the same as the rest of them,' she spat. 'You can't be trusted. You'd screw me over at the drop of a hat.' Shirley took a step forward.

'I don't know what you're talking about.' Kim stood, holding up her hands in front of her, defensively.

'You're just like her. You're just like Toni – full of it.' Shirley picked up the wine bottle and held it, ready to strike. 'You all think you're so damn clever. Toni, fucking my husband behind my back. Did she really think I wouldn't find out?'

'You did know …' Kim stepped backwards, away from the deranged woman closing in on her.

'I found out. Stupid bitch was sending him text messages. Subtle, eh?' Shirley roared with venom.

'Then,' her eyes were wild, 'she goes and gets pregnant!' Kim remembered that Shirley couldn't have children and realised why it would have been such an insult. 'I couldn't have Grant leave me for that bitch. If he'd known about the baby it would have ruined everything. So, I answered her text messages on his phone and told her to get rid.'

'Then,' Shirley spat with rage, 'then she has the cheek to say he raped her and she didn't want it anyway. Of all the vicious lies … as if my husband would rape a skank like that. I bet she was begging for it.'

By then Kim had her back to the garden wall and Shirley was still coming towards her, holding the bottle high, ready to swing.

'So I waited. I waited for the bitch to get rid of the brat. I was patient, you have to give me that. I took my time.'

Kim wanted to scream but found that no words would come out.

'It had been so carefully planned. I was sure I'd get away with it, but then Janet had to go and ruin everything.' A flash of genuine sadness crossed Shirley's face. 'The stupid cow had been following me. She had it on film. She'd recorded everything. I didn't have a choice.'

'You always have a choice,' Kim managed to say.

'No. She would have ruined it all. I had to make her shut up.'

'Is that what you're going to do to me, too?' Kim's eyes were fixed on the wine bottle that was glinting in the sun.

'It's not about you.' Shirley shook her head. 'That's what none of you ever get. It's never about you. It's about me.' And with one swift movement she brought the bottle crashing down towards Kim, just as Barrett and Palmer, followed by a number of uniformed officers, smashed down Kim's front door.

Chapter 23

9am 29 June

Shirley had not slept well. The cell was small, hot and uncomfortable. She'd refused the tray of nasty looking food that had been offered to her, as well as the breakfast that had been shoved through the hatch in the door at 7.30am. Her blood-spattered clothes had been taken away by the forensic team and she was wearing blue scratchy overalls.

Kim was thankful that the police had arrived when they did, because the sound of her front door being broken down had briefly distracted Shirley, meaning Kim was able to turn her face as the bottle came down, so it hit her shoulder. The bottle had broken, and she had splinters of glass in her skin as well as a deep cut, but it could have been much worse. Shirley had been handcuffed and taken away while two officers had waited with Kim for an ambulance to arrive. The gash on her shoulder needed stitches.

Palmer and Barrett sat in the interview room waiting for Shirley to be brought in. She had already been arrested for murder and, with the evidence they'd discovered on Janet's iCloud account, both men were confident she would be charged later on that day. The interview was a formality.

When Shirley appeared and sat down opposite them, she folded her arms across her chest and fixed Barrett with an icy stare.

'Mrs Grubb.' Barrett leant his elbow on the table and rested his chin in his hand. 'I think it would be much better for you if you cooperated with us. You are facing a double murder charge, along with one of attempted murder. These are very serious offences and you are likely to be looking at a life sentence. This is your chance to tell us what happened.'

Shirley shifted in her seat and looked across at her solicitor, who gave a small nod of his head.

'What's the point?' She shrugged. 'You think you know it all. Nothing I say is going to change that.'

'You are aware that we have video footage of you killing Toni Jones on Stourbridge Common, on the evening of June twenty-first?'

Shirley's eyes bulged with disbelief. She clearly had no idea such evidence existed.

'What? How?'

'It was retrieved from the mobile phone account belonging to Janet Cox. It appears Ms Cox had been filming you for months.'

Shirley hung her head and let out a long, loud sigh.

'Stupid bitch.'

The solicitor gave an uncomfortable cough.

'So, you see,' Palmer said, 'it really would be better if you just explained everything, in your own words.'

Shirley lifted her head and stared coldly at Palmer. This was his first encounter with a female killer who had not acted in self-defence, and he felt his blood run cold.

'Toni Jones had been shagging my husband.' She put up a hand to stop her solicitor, who was about to advise her to remain quiet. 'I found out about the affair by seeing messages on my husband's phone. He never was that bright. She texted him to say that since their last meeting she had got pregnant, but that she didn't want the baby. She said if he ever touched her again she'd go to the police. I didn't understand what she meant at the time.' Shirley looked sad for a moment, while Barrett and Palmer felt satisfied. They'd suspected that Toni had owned a separate mobile phone, but they'd never found it or been able to prove it. They knew the messages she had sent Grant would have come from that phone because there was no evidence on her other mobile. 'I couldn't have her destroy my life. I've put up with that man for too many years to have it fall apart because of a slag like Toni. I decided then and there that she had to be silenced. I waited until I knew she'd had the abortion and then started to plan it all. I didn't want the abortion to be linked to the murder, so I had to bide my time. My husband may not be the sharpest tool in the box, but I'm no fool.' Her smile was cold and calculated. 'On that day, after the book club meeting, I arranged to meet her on Stourbridge Common. I told her I had a problem and needed to speak to a friend. She was so nosy she couldn't resist. I had it all sorted.' The memory of her strategy made her smile.

Not wanting to interrupt her confession, but eager to find out the significance of the geranium petals, Barrett cleared his throat.

'What was the relevance of the petals?' Palmer leant forward, also keen to hear the answer.

'Oh, that was clever of me, even if I say so myself.' Shirley's eyes sparkled deviously. 'It was to throw you off. I thought, if I made the scene appear staged and odd, that you might entertain the idea that a serial killer was on the prowl.'

Palmer and Barrett shared a look.

'It so happens that geraniums, like a lot of flowers, are symbolic – they mean foolishness. I thought it suited her particularly well. I had to try and cover my tracks. I couldn't have it lead back to me or Grant.'

'Does your husband know you knew about the affair?'

'No. He never had a clue.'

'What did you do with her clothes?' Palmer asked, looking grave.

'Burned them.'

'Why strip her naked?'

'Same reason. Make it look like something it wasn't. Also,' she smiled, 'I wanted to humiliate her. She deserved nothing less.'

'What happened when you met on Stourbridge Common?' Barrett asked.

'I told her I knew about the affair and the abortion. She looked shocked. I enjoyed that. She thought she was so clever, that she could get away with acting how she wanted.' Shirley spat the words. 'Then she decided to cry rape. Said Grant had come to visit her at home and said he wanted to start the affair again. Toni told me she'd said she wasn't interested and that he had then forced himself on her. Lies. I'm sure of it. All more lies.'

Barrett and Palmer looked at each other, both thinking that Shirley was as deluded as she was dangerous.

'So,' Shirley turned to her solicitor, 'I told her she was a lying bitch and then I caved her head in.'

'What did you use?' Barrett couldn't believe his luck, getting a full confession.

'A cliché, I know,' she grinned, showing a mouthful of white teeth, 'but I used a wrench. Did the job.' She smirked. The solicitor put down his pen and shook his head. There was nothing he could do to help her now.

'And Janet Cox?' Palmer pressed.

'Oh, Janet.' Shirley shook her head with disappointment. 'Poor Janet. She had always followed me round like a lap dog. She turned up at my house that night and asked me to go for a walk with her by the river. It was hot and I was pleased to get out, so I went with her. Then she told me she'd seen me kill Toni. I didn't have a choice. I had to silence her.'

'You are aware she did not come to the police with that information?'

'Yeah, she told me she wasn't going to tell anyone, but I couldn't take the risk. She was acting all strange. Kept saying she'd do anything for me and I could trust her.'

'She didn't mention the recordings?' Barrett asked, keen to know why Shirley had been so careless with Janet's phone.

'No.' Shirley stiffened. 'She didn't tell me about the videos. She said she loved me and that she'd do anything for me.' A look of disgust crossed her face.

'I picked up a dead branch and hit her with it, then pushed her into the water.'

Shirley knew her fate was sealed. There was no point pretending anymore. She wanted to be heard. She wanted them to understand.

'I hadn't planned to hurt her. She made me do it. I didn't have a choice.'

'I see,' Barrett said, feeling a wave of relief that the case was now solved.

'One final question, Mrs Grubb, do you know anything about this?'

Palmer slid the note across the table.

'Yes, I do.' Shirley's expression gave nothing away.

'Had you planned on hurting Mrs Martin? Was that part of your plan?'

Shirley smiled. 'I think I've said everything I want to say for now.'

Chapter 24

12.30pm 19th July

Amy couldn't wait for Johnny to come home. She'd spent the morning cleaning the house and food shopping for all his favourite things. The doctors had told them that he was making an excellent recovery, but he'd need to take things easy for a while. After the last few weeks Amy thought that sounded like a very sensible idea.

As a thank you to Maggie and Marion for all their support, Amy had invited them over for lunch before she was due to drive up to Nottingham to collect Johnny.

The table was laid with a platter of cold meat, various cheeses, some bread and a salad, and she sat awaiting their arrival with anticipation. She and Johnny had done a lot of talking over the last two weeks and had come to a number of decisions, one of which involved Marion and Maggie.

When the ladies arrived, Amy opened the door and greeted them warmly.

'Come through. Lunch is on the table,' she beamed.

'Oh, what a lovely spread!' Marion exclaimed as she entered the kitchen. 'You shouldn't have gone to all this trouble.'

'It was no trouble,' Amy insisted as her friends took their seats. 'I'm so glad you could make it.'

'Well, I've been looking forward to this.' Maggie eyed the fresh loaf of bread. 'We can all relax now that it's over.'

'I invited you both to lunch because I want to ask you something.' Amy's eyes were smiling. 'Johnny and I have been talking and we'd love it if you would both consider being the baby's godmothers.'

Maggie leapt out of her seat and gave her friend a big hug.

'I'm going to spoil that kid rotten,' she promised.

Marion sat quite still, her eyes pricked with happy tears.

'Oh, pet,' her voice quivered, 'it would be my honour.'

'Wonderful! That's decided then. Thank you both. You don't know what it means to us. I can't wait to tell Johnny,' Amy said, resting her hand on top of Marion's. 'Right, now that's decided, let's have lunch!' She reached for the bottle of sparkling water on the table and offered it to her guests.

'I still can't quite believe it.' Marion shook her head, changing the subject. 'Shirley, a killer.' The women hadn't really had an opportunity to discuss it since the news had broken.

'I know,' Maggie agreed, sinking her teeth into a slice of the white bloomer. 'I never liked her much but I didn't think she had that in her.'

'Some people will stoop to any level to get what they want,' Amy added thoughtfully.

'And poor Janet,' Marion added.

'I know. Did you know she was gay?' Maggie turned to Amy.

'I didn't have a clue. I knew she wasn't really interested in men but I never gave it much thought.'

'I still don't quite understand what that's got to do with it,' Marion said, looking perplexed.

'Janet was in love with Shirley,' Amy explained. 'She'd been following her and recording her for months. I hear the police found hours and hours of footage on her phone.'

'Well I never,' Marion said, reaching for some ham.

'Seems Janet recorded Shirley killing Toni. Stupid woman was so infatuated with her that she didn't tell the police, but when she told Shirley she knew what she'd done, that was it.'

'I wonder why Janet told Shirley she'd seen her killing Toni?' Maggie asked.

'Janet was so besotted she probably told Shirley that she'd keep her secret, and thought it would bring them closer. Who knows,' Amy said.

'Shirley knows,' Marion said as she buttered a piece of bread. 'But from what I've heard, she's refusing to cooperate with the police now.'

'How do you know this?' Amy asked.

'I called Grant to see if he and the girl were alright. He sounded awful. Probably feels responsible.'

'He should have kept it in his pants,' Amy said, quietly.

'You know the police are investigating him too, for the alleged rape of Toni?' Maggie added.

'Yes, I know.'

'They think she was responsible for the threatening note I received too,' Amy added.

'My, my, what a pickle.' Marion put down her knife and looked across the table at Amy. 'At least it's over now.'

'I don't think it will ever be over for Shirley.'

'I hope not,' Maggie added. 'She always was a jealous cow. She got what she deserved in the end.'

'And what about Toni and Janet – did they get what they deserved?' Amy asked. 'None of us are perfect.'

'Well, you might not be ...' Maggie winked, lightening the mood.

'What's done is done. Everyone pays the price for their mistakes in the end,' Marion mused, and Amy thought back to the crash Johnny had been involved in.

'Do you believe in karma?' she asked her friends.

'I do,' Maggie spoke with a mouthful of bread and cheese. 'What goes around and all that.'

'And you?' Amy turned to Marion.

'I don't know about that. All I know is that there are good eggs and bad eggs in this world. You need to pick your friends carefully.' She sighed, wishing she'd followed her own advice and never got involved with the book club.

'I'm pretty sure I've chosen wisely.' Amy smiled at Marion who blushed and looked down at her plate.

'Anyway, how are you doing, pet?' she asked, her blue eyes twinkling kindly.

'I'm good.' Amy put her hand on her pregnant belly and looked down at it. 'Everything is just fine.'

THE END

ACKNOWLEDGEMENTS

I feel it is worth adding that I love book groups. I've met some really wonderful friends through a number of groups, and for that I will always be grateful. This book was intended to be more a look at human nature, rather than anything else. It seemed to me that a book club would be an interesting setting, since the people who come together may only have a love of books in common and not much else.

Firstly, I need to thank Andrew Barrett for tirelessly sharing his forensic expertise with me, and Kerry Richardson for being kind enough to help me with the police elements of the novel.

A special thank you has to go to my wonderful beta readers – Alexina Golding, Anita Waller and my mother. You helped me shape this book into something I am proud of.

I am also indebted to my editor, Joanne Craven, for all her hard work on getting the manuscript polished, and the proofreaders who've had to correct all my daft mistakes.

During the writing of this book, on various occasions, I have asked fellow Bloodhound authors to help me out. I am honoured to work alongside a bunch of truly lovely, knowledgeable, and talented people. Thank you all.

Made in United States
Orlando, FL
02 July 2023

34694690R00131